"Accident!"

The word exploded out of me so loudly that everybody in the hall stopped to stare. "It was no *accident*," I cried. "Waring murdered Harris, and I can't believe you're sticking up for him."

"I'm not *sticking up* for Waring," Mel retorted. Her cheeks were turning pink, and she sounded embarrassed and scared. "I was just repeating what some people are saying, that's all."

I wanted to say that she must believe what "people" said or she wouldn't repeat it, but the shock of Mel's betrayal had tied my tongue. "You're supposed to be my friend," I whispered.

"I *am* your friend. I'm just saying that Waring must've been so scared he couldn't think straight—"

"Hell, the poor guy didn't do anything that bad." Damon Ying had stopped next to me. "After all, it was only an Asian who got shot. Lots of *them* around, right?"

Melanie had gone brick red. "I never said that!"

By Maureen Wartski
Published by Fawcett Books:

BELONGING
DARK SILENCE
THE FACE IN MY MIRROR
CANDLE IN THE WIND

CANDLE IN THE WIND

Maureen Wartski

FAWCETT JUNIPER • NEW YORK

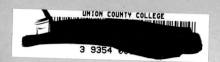
A Fawcett Juniper Book
Published by Ballantine Books
Copyright © 1995 by Maureen Wartski

Library of Congress Catalog Card Number: 95-90141

ISBN 0-449-70442-4

Manufactured in the United States of America

First Edition: August 1995

10 9 8 7 6 5 4 3

For those we have lost to bigotry,
ignorance, and despair.

ONE

When I was a little kid, I used to love the sound of rain. I even wrote a poem about raindrops tap dancing against the eaves, which got "published" in the book our kindergarten was making. Alice laughed herself sore at my poem, but Harris liked it.

Harris ...

Nowadays when it rains, all I can think about is Harris's party. It poured that night and the outflow from the gutter near the kitchen door sounded like Niagara Falls.

Inside the kitchen, Alice and Mitch and I were making egg-salad sandwiches. "I don't know why we're making all this food," I said. "Nobody's going to come in this weather."

"Anyway, we're out of mayo." Alice slapped down the sandwich she was making and added irritably, "For crying out loud, Mitch, *peel* the eggs, don't mutilate them."

"You're just mad 'cause you got stuck with this job and can't hold hands with Len." Our kid brother picked up two spoons from the table and began a drumbeat that matched the drip of rain falling from our eaves.

Just then Dad poked his face around the kitchen doorway. He was wearing a neat white-and-gray striped sport shirt with an alligator on the pocket and new gray slacks, and his dark hair was carefully parted and slicked back. Even from where we stood, he smelled of English Leather.

1

"Why aren't you children dressed?" he wanted to know.

Alice was almost twenty and a sophomore in college. I was fifteen, and even Mitch, at eleven, was no Munchkin. But as usual Dad acted as if we were collectively in the second grade.

"We were finishing the sandwiches when we ran out of mayo." Alice held up the empty jar for our father's inspection.

Dad's forehead wrinkled, and I could guess his thought: why hadn't there been enough mayonnaise in the first place? Aloud he said, "The solution is easy. Wenstein's Convenience Store will have mayonnaise. I'll go right away."

Actually, what he said was, "The sorution is easy." Our dad had been an American citizen for more than twenty years, but he still couldn't manage those *l*s. It was, he'd once explained, because there was no sound like *l* in Japanese phonetics and his tongue hadn't been created to curl around anything so contrary. Until I was four I really thought Mom's real name was "Rora."

"You're not going anyplace, Jun Mizuno," Mom called from the top of the stairs. "You need to set up the drinks and be on hand when the guests start coming. Perhaps Len will go to the store for us."

Mom was about five feet in her socks and on the losing side of a hundred and twenty pounds. In high heels, which she rarely wore, she almost came up to Dad's shoulder. Now she trotted briskly down those stairs and into the kitchen and started taking inventory. "Veggies, dips, fruit tray, cold cuts, and potato salad. You kids are okay."

"The sandwiches aren't done," Alice pointed out. "I'll go to the store with Len."

"No—better get dressed, hon, it's getting late." Mom's glance switched to Mitch's eggy T-shirt, which proclaimed "Animals Are People, Too," and winced.

2

"Mitch, put on a *real* shirt for once, okay? And—where are you going?"

Mitch said he was just going to check on Cheech and Chong. "Not in this rain," Mom objected.

"Your rabbits are fine in their hutch," Dad said. "Listen to your mother and put on some decent clothes. Remember that this evening is in your brother's honor."

When our dad said "honor," his dark eyes gleamed, and his nostrils flared. He looked just like one of those Hollywood-ninja types just before they start to single-handedly whip a hundred and twenty bad guys with their bare hands. "Being accepted with a full scholarship to Harvard is an honor," Dad added, rolling the word lovingly off his tongue.

"I'll go ask Len to go to the store." Alice delicately rinsed her hands and made one of her graceful, gliding exits. Dad watched her appreciatively.

"Alice reminds me of the way you looked when we first met, Laura."

Mom laughed but looked wistful, too. "Selective memory, Jun. I never had a figure like that."

"You always were just right."

My folks smiled at each other, and in spite of the cold April rain drumming down outside, it felt warm and comfortable in the kitchen. Mitch spoiled it by arguing, "*Why* can't I go outside? Cheech and Chong're frightened, I bet. Maybe they're drowning or something." Mom shook her head, and he added craftily, "But I have to. Dad, you always say a man has to live up to his responsibilities."

The buzz word worked. Dad said, very well, just for a minute. Mom cried, "Take the umbrella," a command which Mitch naturally ignored. As rain gusted in after him from the half-open kitchen door, Mom fretted, "That foolish child will catch pneumonia. Terri," she added to me, "you'd better get dressed. We'll do the sandwiches together later when Len comes back from the store."

3

But Len didn't seem in too much of a hurry to get going to the store or anyplace else. As I headed up the stairs, I could hear him talking to Alice in the den. "I'd rather stay here with you," Len was murmuring. "Do you know you look like a flower tonight?" Alice said something I couldn't catch. "No, I mean it. You're like a—a chrysanthemum."

A chrysanthemum with my sister's petite grace, its creamy petals unfolding against the rain—the image was so intriguing that I didn't see or hear Harris hurrying down the hall until we collided.

Harris said, "Ow," and rubbed his forehead. "Terr," he complained, "you've got a wicked hard head."

"Likewise," I told him. My own head had got whammed in the collision because I was almost as tall as my big brother. Alice was the only one in the family who was petite like Mom. Harris, Mitch, and I had Dad's long bones. Mitch was just growing into his inches, and on Harris Dad's height and narrow, high-cheekboned features looked fine. They made *me* feel overgrown and awkward, like a milkweed that had shed its leaves.

Which brought on another image. If Alice was the chrysanthemum in the family and I was a milkweed, Harris was like a sunflower. He wasn't what you'd call handsome, but he had a smile that could light up a room. You couldn't help feeling good when you were with him.

Why that was, I had no idea, but the feeling seemed pretty universal. Harris had more friends than a wildflower patch in June has bees. Adults enjoyed talking to him, teachers enthused over him, older kids respected him, and younger kids worshiped him because he never laughed at them.

In Harvard, Harris was going to study political science, which was just fine, since everybody who knew him believed he'd be secretary of state one day.

Right now he was feeling the top of my head. "You're raising a bump," he was saying. "I'll get you

4

some ice." I said, no, leave it alone, I was okay. "Has anybody come yet?" he then wanted to know.

I said not yet. "But you'd better get down there. You're the guest of honor."

My brother winced. "Don't," he begged. "You should have heard Dad doing the Japanese Thing. Talked about honor, talked about never disgracing my ancestors. I tell you, Terr, I broke into a cold sweat."

He plumped down on the top stair, and I sat beside him. Having been on the receiving end of those ancestor talks on many a report-card day, I could sympathize.

"The whole darn world's coming." Harris sounded more resigned than happy. "The neighbors, Dad's boss, the people he works with, and the people Mom works with, and all the folks' friends." I reminded him that *his* friends would be there, too. "And they'll be hungry," we both said at the same time.

"Dibs!" I shouted, but Harris was quicker and got the word in first. A wicked gleam lit his dark eyes, and I sharpened my brains to meet the challenge of a game we'd played since we were kids.

"O-kay!" Harris leveled a finger at me. " 'Hunger' is the word. 'There is no sauce in the world like hunger,' " he quoted gleefully. "You let yourself in for that one, Terr! My share of tonight's dirty dishes are *all* yours."

"No way, because I know where the quotation comes from. Cervantes wrote that." As my older brother's face fell, I gloated. "You're losing it, Harris. Okay, now it's my turn. We're still with the word 'hunger,' so try this: 'We ate when we were not hungry, and drank without the provocation of thirst.' "

My brother wrinkled his forehead and scratched his head, which immediately caused his hair to rumple hopelessly. "Roger Bacon?" he hazarded.

"Not even close," I chortled. "Jonathan Swift. Guess who's doing the dinner dishes now."

"Foolish children." My dad was standing at the foot

of the stairs and looking up at us. "You are both empty in the head," he added indulgently. "Especially you, Harris."

But he glowed as he said it, and we all knew he was doing what we kids called the Japanese Thing: when Dad felt proudest of his bright, popular son, he shrugged it off and acted as if it was no big deal.

Just then Len and Alice came out of the den. They were holding hands, but when they saw Dad, they unlinked at once. Len said solicitously, "Is there anything you need at the store besides mayonnaise, Mr. Mizuno?"

I had to hand it to Len Kamemoto—he knew how to play people. The first time Alice had brought home this rugged, handsome junior on semester break, our dad had met Len looking like Old Stone Face himself, prepared to loathe, reject, and repudiate any college junior who dared to date his pretty daughter. By the time the visit was over, though, he and Len were buddies and watching awful C-grade westerns together. "Macaroni westerns," Dad called them.

"You don't know your way around town," Harris told Len. He pushed up from the step we'd been sharing and ran down the stairs. "I'll ride along with you so's you won't get lost."

"Harris—" Dad began, then stopped, put his hand on Harris's shoulder, and then lightly touched his cheek. "I suppose I can't order a *Harvard* man about," he said, his voice heavy with pride.

Harris winked at me and whistled his way down the hall where Alice was handing Len an umbrella as if she were presenting a sword to her knight. "Drive *carefully*," she murmured and batted her long eyelashes. I watched Len's expression turn almost glassy. "Come back *soon*."

"An umbrella won't do anything in this downpour. Wear your raincoat, Harris," Mom directed briskly. She clip-clopped out of the kitchen and started digging around in the hall closet. "It's pouring

6

outside. We can't have the guest of honor looking like a drowned rat."

While she was talking, Mom hauled out two parkas that looked like they'd been left over from the Civil War. "I'm not wearing that," Harris protested. "We're just going to Wenstein's, Ma."

"It won't hurt them to get wet, Laura," Dad said, siding with the men against the women.

Mom simply held out the parka. Len took his politely and, sighing, Harris took the other and put it on. It made him look like some swamp monster.

"Just remember who does the dishes," I warned him. He gave me a wave and gurgled deep in his parka.

Then he and Len left. Alice looked after her boyfriend dreamy-eyed. "The store's only five minutes away," I reminded her.

Outside, Len Kamemoto's old Dodge coughed into life. Alice gave me a superior look and led the way up the stairs to our shared room. "Dad sure didn't make this big a fuss when *I* went to U. Mass.," she said.

Graceful as always, she slipped out of jeans and turtleneck and slid on a blue princess-style dress. It went perfectly with her shoulder-length bob and her porcelain, almost fragile good looks. "Like it?" she asked complacently as I zipped her into the dress. "I got it on sale at Filene's Basement. You should think more about clothes, Terri. Boys look at the wrapping paper first."

I digested this new offering from Alice Mizuno's store of wisdom as I pulled off sweatshirt and dungarees and rummaged in our shared closet for my new slacks. Meanwhile, my sister took a pack of Kents out of her bureau drawer, lit one, and carried it to the window which she cracked open. A gust of wind whooshed in, spattering us with rain.

I told her that her disgusting habit was probably going to kill her and meanwhile would drown us both.

7

"Don't you ever read the warning labels on the package?" I asked.

"I know, I know," she said. "I'm going to quit, honest."

Alice took a deep drag of her cigarette and almost choked as someone banged on the door. But it was only Mitch telling us to hurry up and get ready. "I can smell smoke from out here," he added. "Better douse the weed before Dad takes a fit."

"Listen to it rain," I said, as my sister ground out her cigarette and blew the ashes out of the window. "I hope Harris doesn't come to his own party looking like a drowned rat."

Alice snorted. "If you ask me, it's Dad's party. His firstborn *son* has made good, and he's showing off."

Alice had a point because Dad's standard for his sons and daughters was a little skewed. Mom was a feminist who believed that all her kids, male and female, should be treated equally. Dad said he believed that also, *but*—

Put it this way, it was much easier to be a Mizuno son than it was to be a daughter. Harris and Mitch could goof up on occasion, come home late from a party, say, and get away with it. We couldn't. Also, while Dad insisted all four of his kids excel in school and have real goals in life, Alice and I were also expected to be sweet, gentle, and feminine at all times.

"Dad's been an American citizen for over twenty years." Alice sighed. "You'd figure by now he'd stop doing the Japanese Thing."

I reminded her that Dad hadn't left Japan till his early twenties. He hadn't met Mom until he was twenty-six. And even though he adored her, he still wasn't too easy with the fact that his Laura was a strong-minded, independent lady with a successful career in retail management.

"Anyway," I added, "why should you worry? You can get Dad to do anything you want. It's me that has the problem with him."

8

Just then the front doorbell chimed. "Yikes," Alice went, "I'd better go down. What's the matter with your slacks, Terriyaki?"

It was obvious that my new slacks didn't fit. I'd bought them before Christmas, when I was a couple of pounds heavier, and now they sagged on me. "You don't have any hips, you know that?" My sister eyed me critically for a second and then whipped out a scarf from her side of the closet, inserted it through the belt loops, and tied it to one side. "There. That gives you some style, anyway."

The scarf made me look like a bean pole with a bandanna around its middle. I said so, but Alice wasn't listening. "I *wish* Len would come back," she complained. "I don't like him driving that old clunker of his in the rain. Supposing it breaks down?"

Then, I suggested, they would get wet. Alice looked at me in disgust. "That is *cold*," she sniffed. "When you get a boyfriend—*if* you ever do with that attitude—you'll understand how I feel."

She made another exit just as the doorbell rang again. I raked a comb through my thick, coarse, straight, black hair which I'd cut short last summer, straightened my blouse, and made for the stairs.

Alice was already in the hallway shaking hands with Mr. Winchell and his wife. Mr. Winchell was my dad's boss at ROTA, the Boston-based machine manufacturing firm that, until this year, had maintained a huge plant right here in Westriver. In fact, we'd moved into town because Dad was customer-service manager at the Westriver plant, and even though Dad was transferred to the main office in Boston following the plant's shutdown, we'd stayed on in town.

Mr. Winchell was pumping Dad's hand as I came down the stairs. "Congratulations, Jun," he was saying. "Heartiest congratulations. Harris is a son to be proud of."

"No, no," Dad said, doing the Japanese Thing, "not at all."

"He's a fine, fine boy," Mrs. Winchell enthused.

"No, no. Not at all," Dad repeated obstinately. "A very ordinary young fellow. Not even clever. It's sheer luck he got into Harvard."

Looking bewildered, Mr. Winchell tried another tack. "Your daughters are lovely young women—gifted, too. Alice, you're going to be a teacher, right?" She nodded demurely. "And Terri, I heard you were interested in the law. Are you checking into law schools?"

Everyone was looking at me, and a wave of embarrassment knotted my tongue. I tried to speak, couldn't, and shrugged helplessly. Behind me, Dad shifted his stance, and I could guess what he was thinking: how could someone who was so socially inept expect to stand up in court and face a judge and jury?

"We'll have to see about that when the time comes," was all he said. Knowing I'd disappointed him again, I stood mute and miserable until Mom came up to greet the Winchells and lead them to meet other guests.

Alice rolled her eyes at me behind Dad's back, then went off to carry more sandwiches from the kitchen to the dining-room table. I was about to follow her when the door swung open and our next-door neighbors, the Blankards, came hurrying in.

They were both dripping. "It's Art's fault," Emily Blankard accused in her high, whinnying voice. "He wouldn't take the umbrella. 'We're just a few feet away,' he says, and look at me—yech! Talk about your April showers."

Dad sent me to get a towel. When I came back with it, Emily was saying, "Where *is* Harris? We brought a little something for him. Oh, it's nothing, Jun, please don't even think about it. Not everyone can say a Harvard student mowed their lawn, right, Art?"

But Art Blankard was glaring at Mr. Winchell's back. "I didn't know you invited *him*, Jun," he growled. "That sumbitch has got gall showing his face in Westriver after putting all those people out of work. My brother got the ax when the ROTA plant closed."

Dad looked quickly to see if Mr. Winchell had overheard. "It's not his fault, Art," he soothed. "The decision came from the top. He's not a bad guy—besides which, Tom Winchell's my boss."

Art Blankard said, "I hear you," and then bet darkly that Winchell had got himself a good bonus while his workers were getting pink slips. Dad sighed.

"Come and get a beer, Art," he said, and drew him off.

"I hope Art doesn't start trouble," Emily fretted. "He gets so riled up when he talks about the plant closing." She started toweling herself off, paused to add, "Terri, honey, your parents didn't invite those dreadful Despards, did they? After all they've done to cause you trouble, I told Art, the Mizunos wouldn't be caught dead inviting *them*."

The bell rang again, and several people came in at once, among them my neighbor and friend from school, Melanie Reed. "Those pants look perfect on you," she went.

She truly meant it—which was why Melanie had been my best friend for the two years we'd lived in town. Best friends honestly don't see each other's worst figure flaws.

Not that Mel had many problems that way. She was slim and cute and blond and had big blue eyes that were just now checking out the guests who were already there. "I've never seen the house so full of people," she said. "So who's here?"

Knowing exactly what she meant, I gave Mel a rundown of the boys who'd been invited. Since these were mostly Harris's friends, there was a good mix— musical types, computer nerds, engineers, brains, jocks. Almost everybody in the senior class was either already here or coming—

I stopped dead in the middle of a word. The bell had sounded again, and my heart went into massive overdrive as Mitch opened the door to two guys. Melanie nudged me. "Damon is *so-o* cute."

Silently but wholeheartedly agreeing with her, I watched Damon as he and his friend went over to greet my folks. They then sauntered over toward us. "Hey, pretty girls," Damon called.

Damon Ying, running back for the Westriver Rockets varsity team since he was a freshman and winner of every MVP award known to man, walked on the balls of his feet like a jungle cat prowling its territory. He was tall, dark, and lean, and he wore his long dark hair slicked back and tied at the nape of his neck.

And he was also smiling at us. Under that smile, which began with a deep dimple in Damon's chin, curved up to reveal even white teeth, and then rose till it reached large, dark, almond-shaped eyes, I could actually feel my toes curl as if somebody was using a feather to stroke the soles of my feet.

"This is my cousin, Jerry Cho," Damon was saying, indicating his companion. "He's visiting from the West Coast."

Jerry Cho nodded without saying anything. He was a few years older than Damon, as tall but chunkier. In a square, dark, small-featured face, his narrow eyes were watchful.

"Where's the guest of honor?" Damon asked me.

I explained that Harris had gone to Wenstein's, whereupon Damon said he'd catch me later, winked at Melanie, and sauntered away with his cousin in tow. Encouraged by the wink, Mel followed.

"Daydreaming, Terri?" Alice had come up behind me. "Don't tell me you have a crush on Damon," she went on.

"Are you kidding?" But my face felt hot. Of all the people to guess a secret I'd thought safe from everyone—now, Alice would make my life miserable. "He was just asking where Harris was," I muttered.

"Mmhm," Alice went. "Word of advice, Terriyaki—that boy is not your type. He's a *star*, you know, with a star's temperament and a wild streak yea wide. You wouldn't be able to handle him. I, on the other hand—"

I pointed out that Damon was much younger than Alice. "Besides, you have a boyfriend," I reminded her.

"That doesn't mean I can't look at another man—who just happens to be a *year* younger than me," was the flip reply. "Guys scope out chicks all the time, and what's good for the gander has to be okay for the goose."

She paused, hesitated, then added in a quieter voice, "Don't let Dad get on your case, Terri. Just wait till you get your J.D., and he'll be doing the Japanese Thing all over the place. 'Oh, no,'" Alice mimicked, "'my daughter is not clever—so what if she is the finest attorney in Massachusetts?'"

Before I could comment, there was the sound of wheels in the driveway and, peering out of the window, I saw flashing blue-and-red lights.

A police car. "Ah, rats," I groaned. "I don't believe it. The Despards called the cops on us."

"You've got to be kidding. Again?" Alice exclaimed. "Those people are nutcases."

The Despards lived across the street from us and, as Emily Blankard had hinted, were the nastiest neighbors anybody could have. They were famous for calling the cops whenever anything bothered them, which was practically all the time. "Probably they told the police we were making too much noise," I told Alice, resignedly. "Maybe we can head the cops off before Dad sees them, or he'll be so mad it'll ruin the party."

We skimmed to the door and pulled it open just as a policeman left the patrol car and came up the walk toward us. There was a burst of static from his cruiser as he stepped up to the front door.

13

"Is this forty-four Ferndale Road?" he asked. I nodded. "Does Harris Mizuno live here?"

Alice and I looked at each other, and I felt a sudden tingling, a sense of something that wasn't yet fear. Had Len's car broken down? "Yes, he does," I said. "Is something wrong?"

For a second the policeman just stood there with the rain sluicing off him. Then he said, "I'd like to talk to Mr. or Mrs. Mizuno, please."

"I'm Mrs. Mizuno." Mom had come to stand in the doorway behind me. She put her hands on my shoulder as she went on, "What is it this time, officer? Are we making too much noise? I'm sorry, but you see we—"

"Ma'am, I must ask you to come down to Xavier Hospital," the policeman interrupted. There was another crackle of static from his car, the sound of a faraway dispatcher's voice. "I'm sorry, but there's been an—incident involving your son."

"Involving Harris?" Mom's voice rose with the beginning of real fear. "Do you mean an *accident*? Is Harris all right?"

"Ma'am—" he hesitated, took a breath, then said it. "Your son, Harris Mizuno, has been shot."

TWO

"WHY WOULD SOMEONE shoot Harris?"

"It has to be a mistake!"

Alice and I cried out at the same time. Our voices entwined, shrilled up, and then disappeared into the sound of drumming rain.

"What is this? What do you mean, my son's been shot?" Dad strode past Mom and into the rain toward the policeman. He sounded incredulous. "He just went down to the store."

The cop just said, "Please come with me, sir. I'll take you straight to Xavier Hospital."

"But what *happened*? Can't you tell us how badly hurt he is?" Mom cried. "He's going to be all right, isn't he?"

Once more the policeman repeated, "Please come with me to the hospital, ma'am."

"It's bad—oh, it has to be," Emily Blankard speculated in an uncharacteristically hushed voice. My mind started to scramble around in wild directions. Maybe Harris had interrupted a burglary in progress. Maybe he'd got caught in some kind of drug shoot-out. Maybe—

Mom said, "Oh, dear God," in a choked voice, started forward, then swayed as if she were going to faint. Dad just stood there looking stunned, but Art Blankard reached out and grabbed Mom's arm.

"You and Jun go ahead, Laura," he rumbled. "I'll bring the kids."

As if his voice had unloosed everybody from paraly-

15

sis, people began to explode into talk, explaining things to each other over and over as if they couldn't take it in. Harris had been shot—yes, shot! God alone knew why, or by whom, and nobody knew how seriously he'd been hurt—

Into this commotion Alice wailed, "Len—what's happened to Len?"

I'd totally forgotten that Len Kamemoto had gone with Harris. The policeman cleared his throat, "Mr. Kamemoto was taken to Xavier Hospital, too." Then he opened the cruiser door for our parents.

Dad walked, stiff legged, to the squad car. He looked as if he were sleepwalking. Mom started to follow, turned distractedly back to us.

"Art will bring the children, Laura," Emily Blankard cried. "You go on, now, dear, and don't worry about us. We're all praying for you."

We watched Mom and Dad drive on ahead as we climbed into Art Blankard's sturdy Buick station wagon. Art switched on his high beams and put the pedal to the metal, all without saying a word.

He didn't open his mouth again till we reached the emergency entrance of Xavier Hospital, and then all he said was, "My money's on Harris. He's tough—he'll make it."

All the way to the hospital, I'd repeated a single prayer. Let Harris be okay, I'd promised the Lord, and I would never ever do anything remotely sinful again. I imagine that Alice had been on the same wavelength because she grabbed my hand as we raced for the emergency entrance. "They have to be all right," she whimpered.

Mitch had wrapped himself in tense silence that he now broke. "Maybe Harris is just, you know, wounded, not—"

Not dead. Somewhere I'd read that it was bad luck to talk of death in a hospital. I pinched Mitch's arm and hissed, "Don't say it," so fiercely that he shut up.

The emergency-room receptionist directed us to an-

16

other room where our folks were waiting. In a corner by the window, two police officers were talking in low tones to Len Kamemoto. Len looked stunned, and his shirt was covered with blood.

"Len," Alice yelped and started to cross the room toward him, but Dad looked up sharply.

"Leave him alone," he commanded. "The police are talking to him just now."

"Harris?" I pleaded. My mom didn't react, but Dad replied that Harris was in surgery and that the doctors were doing all they could.

"They have the best technology, the best surgeons." Dad spoke the words firmly, as if trying to convince himself. Beside him, Mom gave a hoarse sob. She looked smaller than ever, scrunched back into the waiting room's fake-leather seat. "Oh, children," she whispered, groping for us.

Her hand felt icy. "A man shot Harris when he went to the door. *Shot* my boy," she repeated, in disbelief. "The bullet lodged near the heart."

It couldn't be real. Mom began to sob, and the policemen with Len straightened up. One of them snapped shut a notebook and said, "That about does it for now. We'll need you to come down to the station to make a formal statement, Mr. Kamemoto." Len nodded, not looking up, and mumbled something I couldn't catch. "Fine," the cop said. "Later this evening would be fine."

He looked toward us, seemed as if he wanted to say some word of comfort, then changed his mind and went out quietly, trailed by his partner. Len stayed where he was.

Alice let go of Mom's hand and ran over to Len, dropped on her knees beside him. "Are you okay? Len, what *happened*?"

Before Len could answer, Dad jerked around to stare at him. "Tell us what you told the police," he directed sternly. "First, what were you doing in the

17

center of town? I thought you were going to the convenience store on the corner."

Len blinked sickly up at us. "The corner grocery was out of mayo, so Harris said, we should drive to the Stop and Save in Hanley. My car started acting up just as we passed the town square, and then we drove past the park onto North Street and through the wooded area where the road curves around and around—"

"What does it matter if the road winds or not?" I blurted. "Who shot Harris? A robber, or a mugger, or what?"

"Waring," our mother said dully. "The man's name is Rodney Waring."

"Have the cops *arrested* him?" Mitch almost shouted, and Dad told him to keep his voice down, this was a hospital.

"Let Len speak," he said. "Don't interrupt."

Everybody looked at Len, who said, "My car died in that wooded area on North Street. We tried getting it started, but it wouldn't turn over. The starter, I think—"

"Never *mind* that," Dad snapped, but Len wasn't to be hurried. As if he were sleepwalking through his memory, he described seeing a house set back from the road, half-hidden by trees.

"Harris said he'd go ask the people in the house if he could use the phone," Len muttered. The pallor in his face had begun to tinge with green as he added, "Harris ran down the road and up the driveway and knocked. Nobody came to the door, so he knocked again. I heard him shouting something. And then the door opened and I heard this, ah, this *blast*—"

Len made a gulping sound, jumped up from his chair, and ran, half-doubled up and choking, toward the men's room. Alice dropped her face into her hands. Mom said in a stunned voice, "This Waring shot my boy just because he came to the door of his house. What kind of monster would do that?"

18

"A criminal," Dad said through clenched teeth. "He'll pay for this. Attempted murder is—"

"Mr. and Mrs. Mizuno?"

The swinging doors to our left had parted, and a green-coated doctor came into the room. He looked tired and sad, and suddenly, everything in the room went quiet. Dad squared his shoulders and got up, stood straight, almost to attention. "Yes," he said. "Yes, doctor."

Mom shrank back into her chair, and Alice put her arms around her. Mitch edged toward me, and we clasped hands.

Knowing what was to come, knowing in my bones but praying, still, I gave God a last chance. Please, I thought, let Harris be all right. Please, *please*—

"I'm sorry," the doctor said. "I'm so sorry. We did the best we could for your son, but we lost him."

"We lost him," Mom kept saying. "We've lost Harris."

Relentless as a dripping faucet, her monotonous voice ate into my brain until I wanted to shake her to make her stop. Mom's blind-eyed screams at the hospital had been terrible, but this low-pitched, dreary, endless grieving in her own house, her own bed, was somehow worse.

"It's the medication," Alice said wearily. She straightened up from arranging the blankets around Mom's chin. "She doesn't know what she's saying, Terri. She'll fall asleep soon."

The doctors at the hospital had given Mom a shot. They'd wanted to keep her overnight, but Dad had insisted we all come home. "My family must stay together," he'd said, and nobody argued with him.

Art Blankard had driven us home. He'd hardly said anything, but when he'd helped Dad carry Mom out of the car and into our house, he burst out, "That sumbitch Waring, I hope they fry him."

Dad had just said, tonelessly, "Thanks for helping us out, Art. You're a good friend."

19

"No problem. No problem at all. You want my help, you know where to ask."

When Art had gone, the house became very quiet. Emily Blankard and the others had cleaned up for us, and all traces of the party had been removed. It was hard to believe there'd even been a party. Hard to believe that a few hours ago, we had actually laughed, talked, teased, flirted. Nothing about what was happening now seemed real.

Unreal to hear Mom's drugged whimpers, unbearable to hear her calling for Harris, over and over. She called to Dad, too, but the moment we'd got her into bed, Dad had shut himself in his study, downstairs, and we knew he wanted to be left alone.

We could hear him pacing in his study now, his footsteps as monotonous and as heartbreaking as Mom's sobs. Our dad was a really private, deliberate person. Unlike Mom, who could think on her feet, he liked to plan everything out in his mind before he did it. We knew that he was trying to deal with what had happened to Harris in his own way, but we needed help, too.

"She really wants Dad, not us," Alice finally said. "One of us has to go and get him."

"You go," I said. "I'd only get on his nerves."

Usually, Alice could get Dad to see things her way, curl him around her finger the way Mom could, but not tonight. "He just told me to go to bed," she reported. "He was looking right at me, but I don't think he even saw me. It's like he's in a world of his own, and he doesn't want anybody else there."

So Dad grieved alone. Next door to us, Mitch slept fitfully, moaning and muttering in his sleep. Alice and I, awake in our beds, listened to Mom's intermittent crying and to the sound of the rain.

"Maybe it's just a nightmare," I whispered. "Maybe tomorrow when we get up, things will be like they always were."

"If only—oh, I wish." My sister propped herself up

on her elbow to add, "Terri, I'm worried about Len. He *saw* it all happen, and—and he's blaming himself for letting Harris go up to Waring's house."

In spite of the medication they'd given him at the hospital, Len had been sick to his stomach all evening. But, a small voice niggled in my brain, Len was *alive*.

If Harris hadn't gone alone—if Len had knocked on Waring's door instead of Harris—whoa, Terri, I warned myself, stop thinking like that right now.

Aloud I said, "It's not Len's fault. It's Waring's. I hope they put him in jail and throw the key away."

But, as it turned out, next morning Rodney Waring was a free man. By ten o'clock he had been arraigned before a judge, had pleaded not guilty to the shooting, been bailed, and released on his own recognizance. Mitch, Alice, and I heard all this on the morning news in a segment during which the newscaster referred to "the Mizuno shooting" as if it were a hit movie newly come to town.

"Waring's gone *free*?"

While we were intent on the kitchen TV, Mom had made her painful way downstairs into the kitchen. Her face looked puffy and pale, her eyes were swollen. "They haven't freed that animal?" she moaned.

Even at such a time as this, our mother looked at me, the future J.D. of the family. "Terri, how can he plead not guilty?" she mumbled.

My folks had given me a book on judicial procedure last Christmas, and I'd read some of it. "It's the way things are done, I guess. Waring's attorney has arranged for bail and got him out of jail. Now the district attorney's office will have to bring an indictment against Waring."

They were all looking at me, so I explained what I'd read in the book—that the D.A. would get witnesses and evidence and present a case to the grand jury. "The grand jury will listen to the evidence and see if

21

there's sufficient cause to hand down an indictment that will send Waring to trial," I added.

The kitchen went still and suddenly cold, and I shivered. I couldn't believe that this could be the same room where we had prepared for Harris's party last night, the room where I'd felt warm and happy and safe.

"*If* there's cause for a trial? But Waring killed my son," Mom sank down in one of the breakfast-nook chairs, dropped her head on her folded arms, and cried. Alice bit her trembling lower lip, and Mitch looked scared.

In a moment we'd all be bawling, so I turned on Mitch. "You'd better eat—you're too skinny to skip breakfast," I said, trying to sound cheerful and brisk. "What are you, all of ninety-six pounds?"

Usually, the reminder of Mitch's scrawniness acted on Mom like a cattle prod. I waited for her to leap into action with offers to cook her baby a nourishing breakfast, but today she rocked back and forth as if she didn't even know any of us existed. I glanced at the closed door of Dad's study, where he'd disappeared shortly after we'd come down to breakfast, and wished he'd come out and at least try to comfort Mom.

Alice said she was going to see if Len was up yet, and left. I told Mitch I'd make him some pancakes. While I was activating the micro, he wandered over to the kitchen window, looked out, and did a double take.

"Terri," he went, "who are all those people out in our driveway?"

The media had started creeping up on our house at six A.M. Throughout the day their numbers increased and by noon there were dozens of reporters waiting for us. Because Mom was obviously not up to it, Dad had decided to take Alice and me with him to choose Harris's casket, and as we embarked on this grim mission, I glimpsed a TV truck parked just off our property.

22

"Do you feel your son was shot because he's of Japanese ancestry?" one reporter shouted at us as we headed for our car. "Do you consider what happened a racially motivated incident?"

Angrily, Dad shouldered past a newsman who'd stuck his camera almost in our faces. It didn't do any good. TV cameras whirred, necks craned, microphones were thrust forward. Art Blankard came out of his house and bellowed for the reporters to leave us alone, whereupon the press turned on him and started asking *him* questions.

Okay, granted, it was their job, but the media didn't make life easier for us. And on the day of Harris's funeral we were given yet another reminder of some newsperson's unflagging zeal. I'd switched on the small TV in the kitchen to catch the news that morning, when Mitch exclaimed, "Hey, that's our church, isn't it?"

We all stared at the screen, which showed a familiar, white-spired church. "Today," the TV reporter was saying, "young Harris Mizuno will be buried at St. John's Episcopal Church in Westriver. Mizuno was allegedly shot and killed two nights ago by Rodney Waring—"

"*Allegedly*, huh? Like he didn't do it," Mitch seethed. "Like there's a doubt in anyone's mind. No shyster lawyer can get that guy off, can he, Dad?"

"Not if there's justice left in this world," our father said. Then he abruptly told us girls to check and see if Mom needed help getting dressed.

As Alice and I went upstairs, we could hear the TV reporter talking about Rodney Waring. We learned that Waring was pushing sixty and that he worked as a machinist in Boston. He and his wife lived at 459 North Street, Westriver.

We stopped on the stairs to listen, and the reporter went on, "There seems little doubt that this shooting, regrettable and tragic though it is, was not premeditated. There is speculation that the district attorney's

23

office will not seek to charge Waring with anything more than manslaughter—"

The man's voice stopped in midsentence as Dad clicked off the TV set. "Regrettable?" Alice seethed as we continued up the stairs. "Smug, *arrogant* jerk—what'd he say if someone in *his* family got murdered?"

But I wasn't about to diffuse my hate by loathing any news anchor. He was small potatoes. All *my* hate was reserved for Waring.

Waring, who right this moment walked the earth a free man while Harris lay in a casket with all his dreams and promise furled tight within him. Waring who would eat, sleep beside his wife, ride the T, and walk in his garden while our brother turned slowly to dust and our memories of him dulled, and our pain shadowed and gentled. Hate Waring? It was too weak a word.

With a blackness inside me that matched my new, hastily bought dress, I followed my frozen-silent father and sobbing mother into the funeral limo. Reporters were hanging around the edge of our driveway, but Art Blankard, Melanie's father, Mr. Reed, and some of the neighbors kept them away. Not that this did any good since there were more reporters waiting for us outside St. John's Church.

Unbelievable. Outside, in the sun, men and women with cameras and mikes jostled and craned their necks as they shouted questions. Inside St. John's Church, there was quiet and darkness scented with candles and flowers and a standing-room-only crowd of mourners. Dad's boss and coworkers and Mom's friends from work were there. All the neighbors except for the Despards were there. Melanie, red eyed, reached for my hand when I passed her, and I saw she was sitting with several of my other friends from school. Harris's teachers and his assortment of friends, including Damon and his cousin Jerry Cho, sat close to the front of the church.

And there in his open casket my brother lay in his

best dark gray suit and smiled at us through painted lips.

He'd have worn that suit at Harvard. I squeezed my eyes tight shut and tried to think of Harris alive and well, with his rumpled hair and his infectious grin—and couldn't. A sense of panic filled me as the truth smashed home: Harris was gone, gone always and forever. He wasn't coming back.

Unable to bear the desolation of that thought, I refocused all of my energy on hating Waring. While people sobbed as we passed the casket, I fantasized tearing Waring apart, piece by piece. While Mitch sat beside me red eyed and numb and Alice wept, I heard the judge sentence Waring to life in prison with no hope of parole.

After the eulogy we were driven to the cemetery where we each spaded earth onto Harris's coffin. Then, finally, it was over. Numbed and chilled, our family had turned from the raw grave when we heard a rough male voice shout, "Rodney Waring for president!"

Reflexes dulled by grief, I lifted my head and saw a group of about two dozen men standing about twenty yards away. They were a scruffy-looking lot, and several of them had shaved heads. Many were wearing what looked to be flak jackets.

"That Jap ape got what he deserved," one of them hooted. "Serve him right for taking jobs from honest Americans."

The speaker was a big guy with a close-shaven scalp. He was probably the leader of the pack because his fellow hyenas laughed at his wit. "This country is for white people," the big guy continued. "You slant-eyes mongreloids should go back to Asia where you belong!"

"Get *out* of here!" Dad roared, but before he could move, there were pounding footsteps, and a tall, lean, solid body hurtled past us.

Damon Ying wasn't carrying a football, but he was

25

moving faster than I'd ever seen him on the field. Behind him came his cousin.

I'd heard the words "deadly force" often, but now I knew what they meant. Jerry Cho's hands were like slicing knives, and his feet were weapons. But there were only two of them and soon Damon and Jerry were surrounded.

Dad started toward the melee, but Alice grabbed his arm and hollered at him to stay where he was. Len Kamemoto grabbed Dad's other arm, and Art Blankard shouldered his way up to us to haul Dad back by the waist. Mom just stood there, while I personally had my hands full with holding back Mitch—who wanted to start his own version of *The Dragon Strikes Again*.

"Lemme go," my kid brother shrieked. "You heard what they said, didn't you? I'm gonna *get* them!"

Now a bunch of Harris's friends surged forward to join the fight. "Call the police," I heard somebody shout. "Get the caretaker to call the cops!"

But apparently someone had already thought of this, because just then there was the sound of police sirens. Hearing them, the big, bald-headed guy yelled, "We are *outa* here!" and took off, followed by his limping, bleeding buddies.

As the police squad cars rolled up, I saw Damon standing next to Jerry Cho. There was blood on his white shirt, and his long hair had come free and was blowing in the wind. With his arms folded across his chest, Damon looked proud and defiant, and even at such an awful time, I was proud that he'd stood up for Harris—for us.

"I can't allow those young men to get in trouble with the police," Dad said. "They were fighting for the honor of this family." He told Len to take us home and, in spite of our collective protests, strode over to meet the cops. Alice gave me a poke in the ribs.

"Quit *staring* at Damon," she hissed. "I can't believe

26

that Harris's funeral turned into a—into a free-for-all. Len, I'm glad you had the sense to stay out of it."

Without a word to Alice, Len helped Mom into the limo. Mitch glared at me. "If it hadn't been for you, I'd have nailed that big guy," he accused. "Why did you hold me back, Terri? Why d'ya have to hold me back?"

I told him not to act like a dweeb, but he continued to glower. "I shoulda hit that big, bald guy," he muttered.

"I understand how you feel, but force isn't the answer."

The new voice boomed like a deep bass drum and took us by surprise. Both Mitch and I looked up and saw not James Earl Jones but a tall, scrawny Asian man with a prominent Adam's apple that bobbed above a clerical collar. "I'm Reverend Boris Thanh," he said. "I wanted to convey my deepest sympathy to your family."

Inside the limo, I could hear Mom sobbing, and Alice stuck her head out of the door to ask what was holding us up. I mumbled some words of thanks and found my hand enveloped in a strong grip. "I understand," Rev. Thanh rumbled. "I don't mean to intrude, only to assure you that you're not alone. I represent the Asian Advancement Group." I guess I just stared at him blankly because he smiled, gave my hand another squeeze, and let it go. "Please believe that the AAG will do anything in our power to help you during these terrible times."

In silence Mitch and I boarded the limo. As we started to roll forward, I glanced over my shoulder and saw the cops talking to Damon and Jerry Cho.

"I hope they arrest all those bozos," Mitch fumed. "It's all Waring's fault. I hope he never gets out of jail, ever. I wish somebody'd shoot him."

"Mitch, quit it, okay?" Alice snapped. "You think that kind of talk is going to help Mom?"

But later, when we were back at the house and

Mom had gone up to her room to lie down, Alice came into the kitchen where I was making Mom a cup of tea. She said she was sorry for being short with Mitch.

"I guess we're all stressed out. Where is he?" she asked.

I nodded to the kitchen window through which we could see Mitch sitting by his rabbit hutch. He wasn't doing anything, just sitting.

"Poor kid." Alice slumped down into a chair by the kitchen table and looked at me miserably. "What's happening to us, Terri?"

I shook my head. "One second, we're happy planning a party," Alice continued drearily, "and then—boom!—the sky falls in. Mom totally comes apart, and Dad doesn't hardly say anything, and Len—I mean, I want to talk to him about what he's dealing with, but he won't say a word."

I muttered something sympathetic. "Len's so sensitive, Terri. He *feels* things." Tears brimmed over Alice's eyelids and slid down her cheeks. "And he won't, you know, let me get close to him. He hasn't even held my hand since it happened. He's like, really depressed."

"It's been a really awful day for everybody," I reminded her.

That newscast about Waring. The funeral. The skinheaded goons at the cemetery and the awful things they'd yelled at us. But then I thought of Damon taking those creeps apart, and it made me feel a little better. Better, that is, until I looked outside and saw Mitch sitting with his head hanging down on his chest.

He was crying. "Harris would hate what's happening," I muttered.

Alice nodded. "He couldn't stand gloom and doom," I said. "He couldn't stay mad or sad for long. Remember the practical joke he tried to play on us last April Fools' Day?"

"Who could forget?" Alice actually smiled a little as she added, "He put that water balloon over our door. It was supposed to fall on one of us—"

"And instead, *Dad* opened the door first."

I could picture our brother now, see the horrified look on his face, while Dad stood there with water streaming all over him. My bone-deep tension surged, released into a nervous giggle, and Alice's lips wobbled into a full grin. "Dad l-looked like a drowned r-rat," she faltered.

Suddenly we were both laughing at the memory, laughing with tears in our eyes.

"Stop this at once!" Dad roared.

We hadn't heard him come home, but here he was. He glared from Alice to me, and if looks could have killed, we'd have definitely bought the farm. "How can you *laugh* today?" he thundered. "On the very day your brother is buried, on the day his funeral is desecrated by scoundrels, you can stand here and joke? I can't believe that my daughters could be so unfeeling."

Alice looked stricken. "I'm sorry," I stammered, "we were j-just talking about Harris, and—"

"Two fine young men nearly went to jail because they fought for your brother's honor." Dad was so mad that he could hardly talk. "Your mother is upstairs, out of her mind with grief and pain. And *you laugh!*"

For another moment his furious eyes zeroed in on us. Then he walked away, leaving absolute silence in his wake. "But that's not what we meant," I whispered, feeling evil and slimy. "You *know* that's not what we meant."

Alice didn't answer. Silently, knuckling tears from her eyes, she got up and stumbled out of the kitchen. "Harris," I whispered to the empty silence, "you know why we were laughing. *You* know."

Silence. Nothing—and I rested my forehead against the wall and felt the dull ache under my breastbone

29

grow worse, press harder, until I was sure I would
have to burst open and die. *Wished* I could die—
  Only, of course, I didn't.

THREE

ON THE SECOND day after the funeral, Len Kamemoto testified in front of the grand jury. He was in court for several hours but the grand jury didn't come to any decision about sending Waring to trial.

On the third day, Alice and Len drove back to U. Mass., and Dad returned to work. Mitch and I went back to our classes at the Junior-Senior Westriver High School. Only Mom stayed home to clean up a few things around the house.

During that endless day I dragged my numb self around school and listened as people told me how sorry they were. Everybody was eager to discuss the shooting, and my homeroom teacher assured me that if I wanted to talk, she was there for me, but I was too numb to respond. Luckily Melanie seemed to understand how I felt and was really quiet during our shared lunch period.

When the day was finally over, I was grateful to get home. Here I found Mom still in her bathrobe and sitting in front of the TV. On her lap was an open album of Harris's baby photos, but she wasn't looking at it. Her eyes were fixed on the TV screen.

My normally too-busy-to-sit-down Mom watching a *soap* in the middle of the day? She had to be sick. "How are you doing?" I asked, trying not to sound worried.

"Oh, Terri," she said vaguely, "home from school already?" She dragged her eyes away from the TV and smoothed down her housecoat with a hand that wasn't too steady. "The time's just flown by. I haven't even made the beds."

I said, don't worry, I'd make them. Then, because Mom hadn't started dinner and because Mitch had a spring soccer practice in half an hour, I scouted around the kitchen for tuna fish and onions and a can of mushroom soup. A can of tuna there was, and an onion, but there wasn't any soup to be found.

So I went next door to ask for a loan from the Blankards. *Big* mistake. "I see you're holding the fort, Terri," Emily said. She heaved a sigh that shook her rail-thin frame from head to feet. "It's hard, it's hard. Really, some days I wonder what the good Lord is thinking, sending us these terrible burdens."

Emily had been a big help over the past few days, but her ability to talk circles around any given subject wasn't what I needed right then. I started edging away as she went on, "Your poor mother must be *destroyed*. I'm sure she blames herself for not going to Wenstein's for that wretched jar of mayonnaise herself, as if she could foresee that that awful man would—and did you know that Waring's found a lady lawyer?"

I said I had to start dinner, but escaping wasn't that easy. "Everybody's talking in Westriver," Emily Blankard flowed on. "You hear about the Mizuno shooting everywhere. I was in Wenstein's today and there was a woman who had the gall to say that she could understand *why* Rodney Waring shot poor Harris. If some strange man came pounding on her door, she said, she'd probably shoot first and ask questions later."

A hollow pit was forming in my stomach. "I really have to be going," I said.

"And then Margie Folsom—you know her, she lives on Peartree Road—said that her boy played soccer with Mitch and she knew the Mizunos. Nice people, she said, and what happened was awful, but unfortunately a lot of people were mad at foreigners, espe-

32

cially the Japanese, because of ROTA closing down its plant here and sending machinery to be manufactured overseas."

Emily paused to take breath. "Then Mel Wenstein spoke up and said that made no sense because ROTA's sending their stuff to Mexico, not Asia. What *I* say is that some people haven't got the brains God gave a jackass."

Emily nodded defiantly. I clutched my can of soup, muttered a thank you, and hurried away. Her voice pursued me. "And anyway, never mind ROTA and the economy, Harris was a wonderful boy. Rodney Waring had no call to shoot him just because he was Asian American. That's what I told Margie!"

I ran home and slammed the door behind me, but if I'd hoped for peace and quiet, I didn't get it. The phone rang constantly. Mostly the calls were from friends expressing shock and support, but there was also a lady who called to ask if the floral arrangement she sent us had ever arrived, and by the way asked me questions about the shooting.

During all of this I put together a supper that nobody really ate. Mom picked at her food, Mitch gulped it all down without tasting, and Dad came home late from the office saying he'd already eaten.

"Where's your mother?" he asked. I told him that I thought she was asleep, and he started to walk toward his study without another word.

He still hadn't forgiven me for laughing on the day of the funeral. "Dad," I began, "I want to explain about that afternoon—"

He stopped walking and turned around to look at me so sternly that my tongue seemed to shrivel in my mouth. Everything I'd wanted to say turned to dust, and all I could do was to mumble, "Alice and me—we were j-just so miserable."

He didn't understand—how could he, when I couldn't get out the words to make him see? I could feel a wall sliding down between us, hated it, but

33

could only stand there helplessly as Dad said, "I have work to do. Good night, Terri."

That was how the third day ended. The fourth day after the funeral started out with dark clouds that promised rain and a wind that would whip any umbrella to shreds. Dad had long since left for work and Mom was still brooding over her morning coffee when Mitch and I left the house and trudged to the bus stop.

"No spring soccer practice today for you, looks like," I commented.

"Nah." Then, casually he added, "I don't know's I'll go on with soccer. It's a waste of time."

"Say, what?" I demanded. Mitch had worked like a dog to play halfback this year on the junior high team. He loved soccer almost as much as he loved his rabbits.

"I mean," Mitch went on, "the coach is for the birds. He yells at us all the time, and the kids I play with are jerks." He kicked at a rock with the toe of his sneaker. "I might as well be doing something else."

"Like what?" I asked, and he said he had a couple of things in mind. "You and Tommy aren't going to go into business making dinosaurs?"

It was an in joke. Tommy Reed and Mitch had been friends for as long as Mel and I had been, and both boys had ten thumbs. One time they'd had to make papier-mâché dinosaurs for a science project, and our entire basement had been plastered with paper and glue.

"Nah," Mitch said, kicking rocks again. "I mean, I have things to do by myself."

Just then Tommy and Melanie came up to the bus stop. Tommy waved at us and said hi, but Mitch didn't respond.

I asked Melanie if our brothers'd had a fight, and she said she didn't know and anyway there were other things to worry about. "Are you ready for that algebra test we have second period?" she asked.

34

Of all subjects in school, algebra was my least favorite. I spent first period with the algebra book propped open on my lap, and on my way to the math wing I was still babbling equations to myself. Then I heard Melanie say, "It's really terrible."

I looked up to see Mel standing in front of our classroom. She was talking to a group of kids, and her back was to me. "Harris was a super guy," she went on.

There was a chorus of agreement, and a girl said that she despised Rodney Waring and that he should be locked up and never again see the light of day. Then Mel said, "Yeah, but in a way I can understand how come he acted the way he did."

I stopped dead in my tracks. Mel went on, "Look, it was pouring that night and Harris was wearing a parka with a hood that covered his face. I guess he went running toward Waring's house and pounded on the door, and—well, I can see how Waring thought Harris had come to attack him."

"So why didn't he just call the police?" a boy asked. He was a reed-thin kid with a sandy cowlick of hair that kept falling over his glasses. We had a biology class together, and his name, I remembered vaguely, was Nick Kawalsky.

"*Why* should Waring take out a gun and shoot Harris?" Nick Kawalsky went on. He spoke in a calm, methodical way as if he were processing his ideas along the way. "Harris was outside the door, right? The door was locked, and Waring was inside. There wasn't any immediate danger to him."

"He was scared. That's why he went to get the gun—"

"If he had time to go get his gun, he had time to phone the police," Nick Kawalsky pointed out.

"I'm not saying Waring was right," Mel said. She sounded annoyed. "All's I'm saying is that it's understandable. It was a really awful accident—"

"Accident!"

The word exploded out of me so loudly that everybody in the hall stopped to stare. "It was no *accident*," I cried. "Waring murdered Harris, and I can't believe you're sticking up for his murderer."

"I'm not *sticking up* for Waring," Mel retorted. Her cheeks were turning pink, and she sounded embarrassed and a little scared. "I was just repeating what some people are saying, that's all."

I wanted to say that she must believe what "people" said or she wouldn't repeat it, but the shock of Mel's betrayal had tied my tongue into knots. "You're supposed to be my friend," I whispered.

"I *am* your friend. I'm just saying that Waring must've been so scared he couldn't think straight—"

"Hell, the poor guy didn't do anything that bad."

I looked up outraged, disbelieving, and saw that Damon Ying had stopped a few feet from us. "After all, it was only an Asian who got shot. Lots of *them* around, right? They don't even look American."

Melanie had gone brick red. "I never said that!"

"Maybe you thought it. Morons like Link Lewis are broadcasting stuff like that all around school," Damon jeered. "Why shouldn't you get on the bandwagon?"

Ignoring Mel and the others, he sauntered up to me, slid an arm around me, and drew me away from the others. "You're not going to cry, are you?" he asked.

I wasn't going to give Melanie the satisfaction of seeing me in tears. With an effort I shook my head, and Damon squeezed my elbow approvingly.

"You've got pride—I like that. Don't listen to what fools say, Terri. They don't know squat."

I gulped hard. "Mel is my best friend," I muttered.

"She's not your friend. People are either for us or against us." Dark eyes, bold and sparkling, swept over me and, even at such a time, that look left me feeling weak at the knees. "She shouldn't mean anything to you. She'll never understand how you feel."

"But she knew Harris," I whispered. "She *liked* him."

36

"That wouldn't stop her from taking sides. People always do." Damon shrugged.

Suddenly, as they say, light dawned. If Melanie thought the shooting was an accident, why wouldn't her kid brother think so, too? "So that's why Mitch doesn't want to play soccer," I muttered.

"Life isn't pretty, know what I mean? But, like Jerry says, we don't have to take any crap, either."

Remembering how Jerry Cho had gone after those goons at the cemetery, I didn't doubt it. "Listen, about the day of the funeral," I began, but he stopped me.

"Forget that, okay? What I did was for me as much as for Harris. I hate racists worse than lice."

The buzzer sounded just then, and I had to hurry so as not to be late for that test. But in spite of my hurry, two thoughts followed close.

One of them was that Mel and I were no longer friends. The other thought was that for the first time in my life, Damon and I had really talked. And even more strange and wonderful, he understood how I felt. It was almost as if I *mattered* to him.

"I wanted to meet with you so that we could get to know each other," the short, stubby, assistant district attorney told us. "I'll be leading the team prosecuting Rodney Waring."

Mr. Kurt Shih wore a navy-blue suit and a pin-striped shirt, and his black hair had been cut and styled recently. I'd noticed when he shook my hand that his nails had been manicured.

In contrast to his well-groomed appearance, the A.D.A. had a rapid, forceful way of talking. His movements, like his speech, were almost jerky, as if there was more tense energy in him than he knew how to handle.

"The newspapers have labeled this a racist shooting," he went on. "So be it. It's time the world learned that Asians refuse to be victims. We intend that Waring pay for his crime."

Almond-shaped black eyes watched us sternly from the other side of a desk that was cluttered with papers, files, letters, and memos. There was also a single photo in a silver frame—a pretty, smiling little girl with shiny black bangs. Her arms were around the neck of a huge Saint Bernard.

"Nice dog," Mitch said wistfully.

Sidetracked, Kurt Shih blinked, and for a second the tension almost left his eyes. "Elmo," he said. "Full name, Saint Elmo's Fire. Got a pedigree longer than my arm. He and my daughter are like this." He held up two fingers locked together.

"I have rabbits. I *wish* I had a dog," Mitch said, "but my mom is allergic to dog hair. That's why we have to keep Cheech and Chong in a hutch outside—"

"We did not come here to talk about animals," Dad interrupted. An impatient muscle in his cheek bunched as he added, "What is happening with the trial, Mr. Shih?"

"We are charging Rodney Waring with murder in the second degree," the A.D.A. said. "No trial date has been set as yet, however."

"Will you be able to get a conviction?" Dad demanded. "There's been so much in the newspapers and on TV. There's speculation that Waring's attorney will try to cut a deal. That he'll be given probation for butchering my son."

Silence followed those explosive last words. In that stillness Mom stared down at her tightly clasped hands. Mitch shifted from one foot to the other.

"It won't happen that way. We won't accept a reduced charge." Kurt Shih jabbed a stubby finger in our direction. "Murder two carries a lot of years, Mr. Mizuno. A lot of years. Not that Grace Fallister won't try every trick in the book to get her client off. Have you heard of her, by the way?"

My parents looked blank. All they knew was that Waring had retained an attorney by that name. However, I'd done some research on Ms. Fallister.

"She defended Andrew Brinkell, the man suspected of killing his entire family in Pennsylvania," I said. "She got some crucial evidence ruled inadmissible and actually got Brinkell acquitted."

Dad looked at me in surprise, and Mom's sunken eyes brightened a little. "Terri's going to be an attorney," she explained to Mr. Shih. "She's very interested in the law."

To be truthful, I'd read the *People v. Andrew Brinkell* case attentively only because I wanted to know all about Waring's attorney. What I'd read hadn't been reassuring—Ms. Fallister was tough, smart, and not afraid to play dirty pool.

"*Can* she get him off?" Dad was asking.

"She'll try," Mr. Shih admitted. "You have to understand that Ms. Fallister doesn't necessarily believe in her client's innocence. She did very well for herself on the *Brinkell* case, got rich on TV and book rights. My guess is that *she* contacted Waring and offered to defend him because it's the kind of sensational case she can milk later."

"You mean"—Mom looked stunned at this new thought—"you mean they can make a—a TV movie about Harris?"

Our folks both stared at Mr. Shih, whose hard face registered distaste. "This is the U.S. of A., Mrs. Mizuno. The public loves any kind of sensational stuff. The more sensational the better, in fact."

Mom looked stricken. "Can we do anything to help?" Dad wanted to know.

"Do as you've been doing. Maintain your dignity and be visible as a family." Mr. Shih paused. "Are you familiar with the AAG?"

My folks shook their heads, but the acronym rang a bell. "The Asian Advancement Group," I murmured.

Mr. Shih gave me an approving nod. "You've got it. The AAG is a Boston-based group—I'm a member myself, one of several hundred. Usually we meet in the city, but because of your tragedy, this Thursday we've planned a meeting at the South Street Unitarian Church in Westriver. You should attend the meeting as a family. That would put you in the public eye and make your tragedy work for you."

"With all due respect," Dad said rather stiffly, "we prefer to keep our feelings private."

"Look, Mr. Mizuno, you have to fight fire with fire. If Fallister makes Waring out to be a saint, you have to be right out there proving differently. And Boris Thanh, the pastor of the church on South Street and this year's AAG president, can be a strong ally. You'll want to meet him."

I remembered the scrawny reverend with the deep-drum voice, but my brain wasn't processing right. The assistant district attorney's terse way of speaking was wearing me down, and by the time we left his office, my head was pounding.

We were really quiet driving home. When we got there, Mitch quickly escaped into the backyard to be with his rabbits, and Mom went upstairs to lie down. I saw Dad head for his study, and my headache worsened. Knowing it wouldn't get any better if I stayed home, I told Mom that I had to go down to the library to study, took my books, and left.

Ferndale Road was at least four miles from the center of town, so it took an hour's hike to reach the Westriver Public Library. This was a tired looking brick-and-stone building that stood across from the equally worn post office, a games arcade, and the South Street Unitarian Church.

A couple of years ago, when we first moved to Westriver, there'd been plans afoot to give the library a face-lift, but with the ROTA-plant shutdown the idea had been scrapped. Today, it held the scent of old books and even older radiators that were trying to bring some heat up against the spring chill. I was heading for an empty desk at the back of the library when somebody said, "Hey, Terri."

It was Nick Kawalsky, the skinny blond boy who'd

argued with Melanie the other day. He made a gesture that clearly meant, sit down, here's another chair.

"Thanks," I said, "but I have to cram for a biology test."

But my ploy to be left alone backfired. I'd forgotten that Nick was in my biology class. He held up a book with "BIO" written on the brown-paper dust jacket and said, "Two heads are better than one, unless you'd rather study alone."

There was no way I could get out of this without being rude. Reluctantly, I sat down and was relieved when Kawalsky went back to studying. I started rereading my notes, but the image of Kurt Shih kept flashing up.

"Enough," I muttered. Nick looked up, and I apologized, "I was just talking to myself."

"Biology tests can do that to you," he sympathized, "especially exams given by Ms. 'Biology is an exact science, so please be exact' Corcoran. She makes my teeth ache."

I tried a polite smile. He said, deadpan, "See, I grind my molars when I'm frustrated. I once wrote this paper for English about Corcoran's biology class being subsidized by money-mad dentists."

This time, my smile was almost real. "You didn't."

"Believe it or not, I got an A+ on that paper. It's easier for me to write than talk," he went on seriously. "The other day, when Melanie Reed was saying all that about Waring, I wanted to say a lot more, but—"

He broke to add awkwardly, "I'm really sorry about your brother, Terri."

Then he dropped his notebook and his pen, which immediately rolled under a nearby stack of books. I watched Nick get down on his hands and knees to excavate for that pen and reminded myself that this was definitely not what I needed today.

I was about to get to my feet and tell him that I'd see him around school, when he lifted his head sharply and cracked it on the lowest shelf of books. "You okay?" I demanded anxiously.

He nodded and sat up, his glasses half off and half on his nose, and rubbed his head. "It's the hardest part of me." He sighed. "Scar tissue. When I was a kid, I fell off so many high chairs and trees and fences that my folks bought stock at the emergency room at Xavier. I think I have an even harder head than Link Lewis."

Link Lewis was one of our school's troublemakers, a big, bronze-headed bozo with the IQ of a snail and the personality to match. "No way," I said. Then I added, "Us Mizunos have been to the hospital a few times, too. All four of us are accident prone—"

Three of us now. The truth of this came out of left field and smacked me as hard as Nick had hit his head. Tears of pain spurted to my eyes, and I couldn't breathe for a second. When the roaring in my ears cleared, he was staring not at me but into space.

"Death is rotten," Nick said.

It was the same message I'd heard over and over in the past week, but there was a difference. Nick Kawalsky's voice was husky with firsthand knowledge.

"My mom died two years back," he went on. "She was driving home from work and a drunk driver, going on the wrong side of the road, plowed into her."

I didn't know what to say. After a second, he said, "Sometimes I hated that creep so much that I'd lie awake in bed thinking up ways to trap him and torture him."

The heavy, dull pain under my breastbone made it hard to breathe. "What happened to him?" I managed to ask.

"Probation. It was the guy's first offense—never been in trouble with the law before." Nick's voice was bitter as he added, "His driver's license got taken away for five years—big deal! In three more years, he'll be back on the road again. Maybe he'll kill some-one else."

I pushed the point of my pen onto the notebook so hard that the paper ripped. "Sometimes," I heard my-self say in a low voice, "I can't stand it. It's like Harris could come home any minute, only he doesn't."

Nick nodded. "I kept looking for Mom to walk through the door. Still do, sometimes."

"I—I keep thinking of that night and going over and over it in my head," I mumbled. "Harris and I used to have this game—when we said the same sentence, we'd yell 'dibs!' and the one to talk first got a chance to throw out a quotation. If the other person couldn't guess it, he had to do the dishes."

Maybe he'd laugh, or look blank? But—"Cool," Nick said. He pushed his cowlick out of his glasses. "So who won most of the time?"

"Harris. He had a great memory and kept *Bartlett's Familiar Quotations* handy. But I got him with one just before he left for the store—"

My voice trailed off. My eyes felt heavy with tears, and the inside of my nose was burning. I hung my head, willing Nick to stay quiet.

As if understanding my need to pull my silence close, he just sat there. After a while he looked up. "All that stuff gets bottled up inside," he said. "I know the way it is. I walked around for months as if I had a stone strapped to my chest until I started writing in my journal." I guess I looked bewildered, because he stopped to explain, "My dad suggested I keep a jour-nal after Mom was—killed."

It was a hard word to get out. I felt the hurt with which Nick swallowed before he went on, "I had to do something or go nuts, so I took Dad's advice and filled this notebook with what I was thinking. Most of the time I was thinking about what I was going to do with the creepo drunk, so I must have sounded like some psycho serial killer. But after I wrote it all down, I felt better."

43

Abruptly, he got to his feet. "See you around school," he said, and took off.

When he'd gone, I stayed staring down at my biology notebook for a while. I could guess how hard it had been for Nick Kawalsky to talk about his mom. Why had he opened up to me? I wondered. And what had gotten into *me* that I'd told this skinny boy I hardly knew all that stuff about Harris and how I felt?

Maybe it was because he'd stood up to Melanie that day. Or maybe it was because I *didn't* know Nick Kawalsky. Since grieving was the only thing we shared, we could speak about the shadows and the darkness inside us. Feelings that even good friends might not want to hear—

Someone coughed at a nearby table, and I shook myself free of thoughts. Then, looking down at my notebook, I realized I'd been doodling all this while. "Until the night Harris died," I'd written, "I loved the sound of rain."

I started to scratch out the words. Started, then stopped. I looked at the stark words again and felt the almost physical push of other words, other thoughts, trapped deep in my brain and desperate to get out.

Nick was right. I had to let go somehow, or I'd explode. What the heck, I thought, I could always tear up what I wrote.

And so I picked up my pen and started a new sentence. "Now I hate the sound of rain," I wrote. "It makes me think of someone crying."

FOUR

WHEN I GOT home from the library, I found my dad on the phone, talking loudly in Japanese. This in itself was surprising since he hardly ever used the language, and besides this he sounded stressed. Mitch wandered out of the kitchen and I asked him what was going on.

"Grandma wants to come for Harris's funeral," he announced.

I stared at him, wondering if he had lost it. Grandma Julie had died two years ago. "What are you talking about?" I asked.

My kid brother puffed out his scrawny chest and tried to look important. "I'm talking about Grandma Sachiko Mizuno. Our grandmother from Japan. Dad's mom."

Behind me, Dad was still talking. Upstairs, I could hear Mom's radio being played very loud—a sure sign that she was agitated about something.

"When did this happen?" I gasped.

"The telegram came while you were at the library." Mitch's eyes sparkled with excitement as he described our parents' reaction to the news. "It, like, blew the folks away. Mom's never met her, even."

None of us—except for our father, of course, and *he* only had one photo of his mom—had ever set eyes on Grandmother Mizuno. We'd never even communicated with her except for the New Year letter we exchanged each year.

Those annual letters, written in Japanese, always

45

arrived in January. Dad's translations seemed formal and without warmth, and anyway she never wrote very much or said anything personal.

To us kids Grandma Mizuno was a one-dimensional character, about as real as a magazine illustration. Still, at Mom's urging, we had always replied to our Japanese grandmother's letter. We'd sent photos of ourselves, too, which she never acknowledged receiving. Once, when I was in second grade, I'd sent her what our teacher said was a very nice haiku: "The morning dew falls, /frogs croak sadly in the pond, /Japan is so far." Grandma Mizuno had never mentioned that poem, either.

After a few tries we stopped expecting anything from our grandmother in Japan. Writing to her had been just another duty—something like being asked to dust the furniture because company was coming.

Now company *was* coming, apparently. "But, wait a minute," I protested, "why come *now*? The funeral's over."

"I guess that's what Dad's trying to explain," Mitch said. We listened in, trying to pick out the sparse words of Japanese we had learned from our father through the years. We heard him say, *shikashi*, which means, "but" or "however" depending on how you use it, and then he said, *komarimasu, na*, which is a polite way of saying that he was feeling royally bummed.

I asked, what did Mom say? and Mitch replied that she was worried that Grandma Mizuno mightn't be able to take the long trip over.

"She's seventy-five, and she's never flown before," Mitch enlightened me. "She's never even been out of Japan."

Just then Dad came stalking out of the kitchen. "Is Grandmother Mizuno coming?" I asked.

"On Wednesday." Dad walked away from us, stubbed his toe on the bottom stairs and swore. In Japanese.

We exchanged glances. "He's really ripping," Mitch muttered.

Dad strode upstairs, and we could hear him talking to Mom. Their voices began to rise, and Mitch and I heard Dad say, "She's my mother, Laura. My widowed mother. I cannot tell her not to come. She says it doesn't matter that she missed the funeral. She thinks it's not too late to light incense over Harris's ashes."

"Say, what?" Mitch asked, bewildered.

I shook my head. Upstairs, Mom was declaring, "I never said that you should tell her not to come. She's Harris's grandmother, and she has every right to be here. What I'm saying is that it may be too much for her."

Mom sounded more like herself than she'd been since Harris died. "How long is she planning to stay?"

"I have no idea," Dad retorted. "I suppose she'll tell us when she arrives."

"Which will be in a couple of days." After a long pause, Mom added resignedly, "Well, I suppose we can convert your study to a bedroom."

But Dad didn't go for that. "The study's too small. Mother can stay in the girls' room."

Mitch nudged me. I pricked up my ears as Mom agreed. "Alice isn't home, so it'll work out fine. Terri can clean out the closet and empty out Alice's bureau."

One thing I can say for Grandma Sachiko Mizuno's visit—her unexpected arrival was like a tonic for Mom. She shed her sleepwalking look and got moving—which meant that she also had us kids working. I had to tidy Alice's side of the closet and change the sheets on Alice's bed. Mitch got the job of scrubbing out the bathroom we kids shared.

"Why me?" he complained, after which Mom gave him a lecture on how clean Japanese people were and how she was personally going to inspect everything in the bathroom. "You mean I have to clean up *every* time I take a shower?" my kid brother then sputtered. "What kind of a person is Grandma, anyway?"

Mom said that we'd have to ask our father that. Being more than a little curious—I was, after all, going to share a room with the lady—I asked Dad at dinner that night about our Japanese grandmother. I had to ask him twice because he seemed deep into his own thoughts.

"I have seen her only once in twenty-five years," he replied finally. "That was when your grandfather died in '78."

Mom nodded. "I offered to go to Japan with your father, but he didn't think it was a good idea."

"Why?" Mitch asked. He pushed back his hair with a gesture that was so much like Harris's that I almost winced. I glanced at Mom and saw that she hadn't missed it—she was biting her lower lip, and her eyes were brimming.

I hate you, Rodney Waring. I despise you. I hope you die—but my black thoughts trailed off as Dad said, "When I left Japan in 1965, my father was so angry with me that he never spoke or wrote to me again." He paused, seemed to sigh. "My elder sister sided with my father. We haven't exchanged a word in thirty years."

"But Grandmother Mizuno writes us every year," I pointed out. "Right, Mom?" There was no response, and I saw that her eyes had started to go dull again. To keep her with us I said loudly, "You always made us answer those letters."

"There's no need to yell, Terri," Dad reproved. "Yes, my mother wrote, even though she's very traditional in her thinking. In her world women do as their husbands tell them. Writing to us once a year was the only time she ever disobeyed my father."

Finally distracted from thoughts of Harris, Mom frowned. "It's disgraceful, what women in Japan have had to put up with. But, Jun, life is so different in

48

America. I wonder if your mother's going to be comfortable here."

Dad said he hoped so. "Does she have to follow any kind of special diet?" Mom's forehead puckered. "Maybe she'll want to have *miso* soup every morning."

Mitch groaned, oh, gross, and Dad said that all this worrying was unnecessary. "My mother won't expect *us* to eat *miso* soup," he pointed out. "*I* certainly don't intend to do so."

Grandma arrived on a Wednesday. On that day we drove forty-five minutes to Logan where we discovered that the connecting plane from Kennedy was half an hour late. When it finally arrived, we craned our necks until Dad suddenly exclaimed, "There she is!" and this tiny person came walking down the carpeted corridor toward us.

Grandma Sachiko wore a black kimono. Her white hair was brushed back from a small, pale, strangely unlined face and caught in a knot at the back of her head. On her small feet she wore split-toed white Japanese socks and black go-aheads. In one fragile hand she carried a small bundle tied up in what looked to be a green scarf.

"*Okaa-san*," Dad called. He hurried over to her and took the small bundle from her. Then he bowed.

Grandma bowed, too, and said something in a voice as thin and as small as herself. She bowed again, even lower than before and then she raised the sleeve of her kimono to her eyes and dabbed at them.

Mitch and I just stood there staring at this fragile little old lady. I don't know what we'd expected—maybe someone more like Grandma Julie, who'd been stout and had carefully groomed dark hair and a laugh that wouldn't quit. Beside that memory Grandma Sachiko seemed like someone from another planet.

Mom gave me and Mitch a nudge. "Go ahead and greet your grandmother," she whispered, shooing us forward. "Bow, like Dad just did, okay?"

49

The little old lady now turned to look at us. Obediently, we bowed and chorused our greetings. Her eyes registered pleasure at seeing Mitch, and then widened as she took me in. "So big girl you are," she faltered.

She had a definitely Japanese accent, much stronger than our dad's, but at least she was speaking in English. Relieved, I smiled at her. "Mom says it's because I eat too much," I said.

"No, no, that is wrong thing to say," Grandma said. Slowly, pronouncing each word with care, she added, "Chirrens must eats lot of foods."

She looked indignantly at our mother who said, "Hello, Mother Mizuno. I'm so glad to meet you at last, even at this terrible time."

She bowed. Grandma Mizuno bowed, too, but I noticed that this bow was not as deep as the one she'd given our dad. *"Hajime mashite,"* Grandma murmured.

Mom looked blank. "My mother just said that it's good to meet you for the first time," Dad translated.

"Ah," Grandma sighed. "You do not speak Japanese. Chirrun speak Japanese, yes?" We shook our heads mutely. *"Arré, ma,"* sighed the old lady.

"You speak English so well." Mom smiled, but Grandma didn't smile back.

"In Japan, chirruns learn English in school. My daughter Mariko's chirrun, teach me how speak English, too." Grandma couldn't manage the *l*s, I noted. She glanced at Dad. "Mariko sends greetings, Juntaro."

It seemed to me that Dad's mouth tightened, but all he said was, "Let's get your luggage, *Okaa-san.* You two help your grandmother, all right?"

Help her to do what? Mitch and I glanced at each other in bafflement while Mom asked how Grandma Mizuno's trip had been. "I'm sorry our oldest daughter, Alice, couldn't come to meet you," she added. "She'll be home from college on the weekend."

"A-ri-su," Grandma acknowledged. "She is big girl like Terri-chan?"

"No, she's small and really pretty," I said, but Grandma Mizuno wasn't paying attention. She was staring at a couple of kids who were deep in a clinch in the airport corridor. Her small eyes went round, her small mouth became a perfect O.

"America may take some getting used to," Mom murmured.

Grandma didn't reply. She peered around her as she trundled down the corridor on her polished Japanese go-aheads. Her shiny white split socks flashed like rabbits' feet under her black kimono, her gray head whipped from side to side. *Arré*, she said as a kid with a punk haircut and a boom box on his shoulder bopped past. She stared bug-eyed as a group of girls dressed in the shortest of miniskirts waltzed by. *Arré, arré, ma!*

We had arrived at the conveyor and Dad stared at the luggage going around the carousel. "Which one is yours, Mother?"

Grandma pointed to a huge suitcase. "That one."

Dad grabbed it, hauled it off the carousel. "That one, too," Grandma added, pointing to a second suitcase as big as the first. "And that one."

The third item of luggage was a bundle of three boxes tied together with string. Mitch pulled them off the carousel and nearly dropped them on his own foot. "That's one heavy sucker," he gasped. "What have you got inside, Grandma? Rocks?"

"Rocks?" The old lady looked shocked until she realized that Mitch was making a joke. She laughed a little behind her small hand and said, "I bring with me *nuka*. To make Japanese pickle, you know? Juntaro likes very much."

She patted Dad's arm and smiled up at him. "Don't know if can get in America *nuka*," she added. "I am bringing *miso* and *wakame*, too. Juntaro like soup very much."

51

Mitch grinned at Dad's discomfiture, and our grandmother beamed at him. "Mitch-chan, Terri-chan, call me *Obaachan*," she said. "It mean 'grandma' in Japanese." We nodded agreement and she said, "When we go you home, Rora-san, I can show you how to cook Japanese food for please your husband."

"Aha," Mom said.

As we wheeled our grandmother's pile of luggage out of the airport, I realized that she'd answered my question. She intended to stay with us for a long, *long* time.

The first thing Obaachan did after we got home was to unpack her clothes. She refused Mom's offer of help and mine, too, so I sat on my bed and watched her carefully sliding out black kimonos, black overgarments that fitted like happi-coats over the kimonos, split-toed white socks and shoes. She then just as carefully laid each garment between white sheets of paper she had brought with her and slid them into the drawers of Alice's dresser.

If her suitcase was any indication, Obaachan had packed for a hundred-year visit. Besides the Japanese kimonos, she'd brought baggy black pants, gray and black sweaters and white blouses, socks and slippers. A black winter coat that reeked of mothballs bulked out the bottom of her huge suitcase.

"America too cold," she explained, as I helped her hang the heavy garment in the closet we would share. "In April, Japan is warm, cherry blossoms already are bloomed. Japan spring more pretty."

My grandmother then went into the bathroom—cleaned again this morning by a complaining Mitch—and emerged in a brand-new kimono, brand-new two-toed socks and go-aheads. "I am ready now," she announced. I looked at her blankly. "Ready to go to the family altar," she then explained.

Definitely bewildered, I led her downstairs where

she told Dad something in Japanese. He replied in English, "We don't have a family altar, Mother."

Obaachan's eyes opened wide as Dad explained to her that American customs were different. "If you wish," he went on in a strained voice, "we can visit the cemetery where Harris has been laid to rest."

Mom lowered her eyes. Obaachan bent her gray head. "If that is the way it must be, it can't be helped," she murmured.

Shikataganai—it can't be helped—became her favorite phrase. She used it whenever she disapproved of anything, and she disapproved of almost everything Mom or I did. Mitch-chan was still a little boy, and she obviously doted on him. Dad was the head of the household, the big boss. To criticize *him*, I gathered, would have been an insult to all the Japanese ancestors.

I'd thought we'd gotten used to what we called Dad's "Japanese Thing," but as I told Alice that evening when she phoned to greet our grandmother and ask me how things were going, she hadn't seen nothin' yet.

"Tonight after dinner, Dad went to plug in the coffeemaker," I reported to my sister, "and Obaachan took a fit. She said that in Japan, the wife takes care of that kind of thing. 'Wife do for husband all comfortable things,' quote, unquote."

Alice said Mom must have come unglued. I said, yes, sort of, but in a subdued way. "She's still not the way she used to be," I told my sister. "She's changed so much since—well, you know."

"We've all changed." Alice sounded depressed for a minute and then rallied enough to joke, "So, you're sharing a room with the old girl. Hang in there, Terriyaki. Remember, Grasshoppah, that cultural knowledge can be gained from generational encounter."

Cheered by a good laugh, I went to bed. Not to sleep, mind you, because Obaachan was up and down all night, rummaging in the drawer, in the suitcase, in the closet, under her pillow. Twice she went to the bathroom and, since she didn't really know the way, got disoriented so that I had to get up to direct her back to bed.

Finally, I fell asleep only to awake to a weird smell floating through the house. It was like nothing I'd smelled before, a kind of wet, slimy, fishy odor accompanied by the stench of something burning.

Fire! I ran out on the landing and found Mom, in her bathrobe, walking up the stairs. "Mother Mizuno is cooking *wakame* soup," she announced. "I think it's made of kelp."

I dressed and, followed by Mitch, went down to the kitchen where the fishy smell was overpowering, and where we discovered that the burned smell came from dried seaweed that Obaachan toasted over the burner.

"Very good for you," she insisted, but Mitch and I took one look at the soup and the toasted seaweed, and got out the cereal. "You mother never make for you?" Obaachan wondered, shooting an accusing glance at Mom. Then, she turned all smiles as Dad walked into the kitchen.

None of us ate any of Obaachan's cooking except Dad, who said later that he didn't want to hurt his mother's feelings. "But it only encourages her," Mom whispered, as Obaachan left the room happily to fetch more soup for Dad. "She'll make us this stuff for breakfast every day." Then she added that she liked Japanese food and knew it was supernutritious, but that seaweed in the morning was more than she could face.

That went double for me. I tried to hold onto my appetite as we watched Obaachan slurp up the disgusting-looking soup and noticed that Mom also left most of her breakfast untouched.

"I'm off to work," she said finally. "I hope you'll get some rest, Mother Mizuno—you must be feeling so tired from jet lag. You'll have plenty of peace and quiet because Terri and Mitch will be at school, and Jun and I won't be back till late afternoon."

"You work in office, Rora-san?" our grandmother asked. "What you do?"

She didn't understand the word "retail," so Mitch and I tried to explain using pantomime. I don't know if we got the point across, but at last Obaachan laughed.

"Mitch-chan, you are funny boy. You remind me of my other grandson, Kenichi. You want see photo?"

We gathered around curiously as our grandmother brought an envelope of photographs from our shared room and spread them out on the kitchen table. We had, I saw with interest, three cousins: a boy Mitch's age and a boy and a girl much older.

"Your aunt Mariko's children," Obaachan explained. "Mariko is Juntaro's older sister."

We'd known that we had an aunt, but Dad hardly ever spoke of her, and we hadn't given her much thought. Now, I looked curiously at the comfortably plump, gray-haired woman and her children.

Obaachan then handed Dad another, older photograph. In it I saw our grandmother as a much younger woman standing behind a stern-looking man in Japanese kimono and wide-legged Japanese pants. There was a kid on each side of him—a teenage girl and a little boy.

"Is that you?" I asked Dad, and he nodded without comment.

I guess the Japanese Thing didn't apply to doting grandmothers, because Obaachan began to brag about our Japanese cousins. The oldest boy was a doctor, she said, the second boy was still in middle school and doing well, and the girl was an "O.L." I asked what that was, and Obaachan said that my cousin worked in an office serving tea and taking messages and so on.

"Office Lady," Obaachan said proudly. "She got good job. Graduated top her class from Kobe College."

"But if she's a college graduate, why doesn't she have a managerial position?" Mom asked. Obaachan looked at her with an expression that showed she was just as bewildered as Mom was.

"Her parents rich. Kazu-chan doesn't have to work. She work in office, then get married. Marriage best thing for girl."

Mom's eyes narrowed, but all she said was that she'd heard that several of Japan's politicians were women. "Even cabinet ministers," she added pointedly.

Obaachan shook her head over such foolishness. "Is influence from the West," she finally said. "*Shikataga-nai,* but it sad. Women all mixed up nowadays. Think they good as men."

Now sounding much more like her old self, Mom announced that *her* daughters were equal to any male. Obaachan sniffed. "What means, equal?" she demanded. "What they do?"

She nodded when she heard that Alice was going to be a teacher, but she looked startled when Mom said I was going in for law. "This is true?" she asked me. "You become lawyer?"

Now that all of them were looking at me, I found my tongue tying into its familiar knot. "Maybe," I said.

" 'Maybe' doesn't cut any mustard," Dad said impatiently. "You can only become an attorney if you're highly motivated and willing to work hard."

"She'll be a *good* lawyer," Mom protested. "Terri is very bright. Why, she and Harris—"

She broke off abruptly, and the house became very still. But before the silence could become painful, the phone began to shrill.

I hurried to answer it and heard a deep bass voice on the other line saying, "Boris Thanh here. Is this Miss Mizuno? I'd like to speak to your father or mother, if I may."

56

Dad took the phone, listened, and said, yes, thanks, we would be there. "What is it, Jun?" Mom asked.

"That was Reverend Thanh, the man Kurt Shih mentioned. He's invited us to attend the Asian Advancement Group's meeting at the South Street Unitarian Church this evening. Apparently Shih's going to be a speaker."

Obaachan had been trying to follow what we said, but we were talking too quickly for her. She picked up on what Dad had last said. "Ah, you are going to meeting," she said brightly. "I will cook dinner for you."

Mom explained, rather hastily, that we would probably eat something on the way to the meeting. "Perhaps," she added, "you would like to come with us, Mother Mizuno."

Surprisingly, Obaachan did opt to come with us. First, though, she made Mitch and me sit down after school to what she called "honorable three o'clock," which was a hefty snack of thick slices of toast with jelly, milk, and a sweet, dense, golden-yellow cake she'd brought from Japan.

She offered the same snack to the folks when they came in. Dad ate a big hunk of the cake, but Mom said it was made with nothing but egg yolks and that she had to watch her cholesterol. "Are you kids ready to rock and roll?" she went on.

Eh, whatszat? I could see Obaachan's puzzlement at Mom's words, and later, as we sat on each side of her in the back of the car, she pinched my arm slightly. "Terri-chan, in America there is dancing music in church?" she whispered.

I said no, "ready to rock and roll" was just an expression. She still looked puzzled, but let it go.

"This is town of Westriver," she murmured to herself. "Juntaro, please to drive slowly. I want see town."

Obaachan needn't have worried since Dad was the slowest driver in the world. As we crawled down the winding length of Ferndale Road, Obaachan admired the big houses and manicured lawns. "So big," she kept saying, "too much space, not like Japan." Then, as we turned past Wenstein's Convenience Store onto South Street, she nodded over the older triple-deckers that were set almost flush with the sidewalk. "More like Japanese mansion," she approved.

Dad explained that in Japan "mansion" meant a condo. "And this used to be the Westriver plant," he went on.

Obaachan's eyes widened as our car crawled past a huge, tree-shaded complex on South Street. "Is close now," she murmured. "So sad. Many peoples have no work. It true?"

Mom said, unfortunately it was. "Luckily, Jun is management," she went on. "The people who were laid off were mostly all factory workers."

As she spoke, we reached the center of town. At first glance Westriver Center looked prosperous, but that first impression faded as you saw that many of the attractive-looking shops lining the street were closed. The Bank of Westriver had a depressed look, and the *Westriver Herald* newspaper office could have used a coat of paint. Even the knot of kids hanging out in front of the Joystick Arcade looked sullen.

The church parking lot was next door to the Joystick. As we swung into it, Obaachan tugged at my sleeve. "What is that place?" she asked.

I told her that it was a video arcade where people played games. Mitch added, "It's a cool place, Obaachan. There's some really awesome games in there."

Before our grandmother could ask any more questions, Rev. Thanh came out to welcome us. Scrawnier than ever in his chino pants and dark pullover, he reminded me of Ichabod Crane in the headless horseman story.

Harris would have shared that thought—I almost turned my head to grin at my big brother, stopped myself just in time. Meanwhile, the reverend was saying, "I'm grieved for you, really grieved. I was at the funeral, but I didn't want to intrude on your grief."

Mom ducked her head and bit her trembling lower lip. "I almost feel as if I've lost one of my own," Rev. Thanh went on. "What I mean is that though I didn't know your son, I've grieved for him—and for you. Somehow we must make sure such a tragedy doesn't happen again."

Dad thanked the reverend and introduced Obaachan. She and Rev. Thanh bowed to each other, and he went, "Welcome, Mizuno-san. We will make sure your grandson's bright candle is not forgotten."

Obaachan looked astonished. "*Arré*, you know that saying," she began, but the reverend was already leading us down the church aisle to front-row seats.

The church was already full, and amongst a sea of unfamiliar faces I was glad to see Damon sitting beside an elderly lady who had to be his mother. Jerry Cho was with them.

Old and young, male and female, the assemblage was made up of Asians, but there were two exceptions. I was surprised to see Nick Kawalsky sitting next to an older man with thinning red hair. Apart from the color of their hair, Nick and the older man looked exactly like each other.

"Reg Kawalsky, editor of the *Westriver Herald*," Rev. Thanh said, stopping to introduce us. As my dad was shaking Mr. Kawalsky's hand, Kurt Shih walked in.

I saw him take one swift look around the place—an attorney's keen, all-encompassing stare. Then he saw us, waved, and started walking slowly down the aisle, talking to people as he came.

"Kurt Shih is an excellent prosecutor," Rev. Thanh assured us. "Fourteen years as an assistant district attorney and one of the most formidable advocates I've ever seen in court. Ms. Fallister had better know her case inside out, because Kurt will tear her into legal pieces."

59

"I hope so," Dad said as the reverend left us. He spoke quietly, but his eyes burned.

In a few minutes, Kurt Shih came up to greet us. "I hope you won't mind if Boris introduces you before the meeting," he said. "Your being here validates what I'm going to talk about tonight."

The meeting now commenced with an opening statement from the reverend who introduced our family and talked about Harris so movingly that there weren't many dry eyes in the church. Mom sobbed aloud. Obaachan sat there with tears in her eyes. Even Mitch was sniffling. But Dad sat tearless, and so did I. Harris's death was too terrible to be relieved by crying.

Where are you, Harris? I asked him in my mind, but of course there was no answer. He was gone, blown away into the rainy darkness because of a trigger-happy demon called Waring.

With an effort I concentrated on Rev. Thanh, who was introducing Kurt Shih as an active member in the Asian Advancement Group and the assistant D.A. of Norfolk County. From what he'd said earlier, I half expected Mr. Shih to talk about Harris, too, but what he essentially said was that we Asians needed to stand up and speak up for ourselves.

"Too many members of the Asian American community don't report hate crimes," he exclaimed. "We who are members of the AAG have to make sure that this doesn't happen. We need to elect Asians to office. We need to make our voice heard in government and from pulpits and in schools. We need to protest what is happening to our own."

He took two steps away from the podium, whipped around and leveled a forefinger at us as if it were a weapon. "Florida: a Vietnamese American is beaten to death by kids who called him 'chink' and 'Viet Cong' while other kids watched. California: five Asian American kids are gunned down by an AK-47 while they're playing in the school yard."

"Horrible," I heard someone moan.

"Houston: eighteen-year-old kids shouting 'white power' murder a fifteen-year-old Vietnamese refugee." The A.D.A. paused to add, "And I haven't even started. Asian businesses burned by arsonists. Vandalism. Gunshots fired against a Chinese American church in Arizona. And right here in Massachusetts, fires and vandalism and shootings. It goes on and on—"

"It'll go on forever. Talking never got us anywhere, and you know it."

I looked around with everyone else. Jerry Cho had risen to his feet. Arms folded across his broad chest, chin thrust at a combative angle, he added, "Talk won't put Waring in jail."

"Identify yourself, please," Kurt Shih rapped out. From the look on his face, I was sure he wasn't at all happy to be interrupted.

"I'm Jerry Cho. I recently arrived from L.A., and shortly after I got to Westriver, the Mizuno boy was shot in cold blood." His voice hardened. "Now I have a question for you, Mr. Shih. Do you really think you can convict Waring of murder two, or are you just out to make political headlines?"

There was a ruffle of noise up and down the church. Kurt Shih snapped, "You're out of line. Naturally we intend to prove Mr. Waring guilty of second-degree murder."

"Waring will cop to a lesser," Jerry warned. "His lawyer will plead it down. It always happens, doesn't it, Mr. Assistant District Attorney? You know as well as I do that Waring will walk."

Now everyone started to talk at once. In the midst of the commotion, Nick's father got to his feet, hitched up his pants, and waved a hand.

Kurt Shih raised both hands, and the noise level died down. "Quiet down, now, people. Let the editor of the *Westriver Herald* speak."

The newspaper editor waited patiently for Jerry to

sit down and for the church to grow quiet. "Is there a likelihood that Waring will plead to a lesser charge?" he then asked.

"No," the A.D.A. snapped. "We won't make any deals on this one."

Jerry Cho jumped to his feet again. "So you say now," he accused. "Well, Mr. A.D.A., you've been giving us a bunch of statistics about Asian victims. Want to hear another for the record?"

I could see Kurt Shih weighing and measuring. He very much wanted to shut Jerry up, but on the other hand this course of action might backfire. Better to let the nuisance have his say. "Tell your story," he snapped.

Still with his brawny arms locked across his chest, Jerry talked about his boyhood in California. His parents, he said, had been hardworking folk who owned a small grocery store in Los Angeles.

"We were well liked in the neighborhood," he told us. "My dad knew all his customers by name, and he gave credit when they needed it. Then, one time, a white man we didn't know and hadn't seen before came to the store. He accused my parents of price gouging, said they were thieves. My dad threw him out."

He paused, looking around the church. "That man belonged to a local hate group called the White Star. That night he came back with his buddies and set fire to our store. My dad was killed, trying to put it out. My little sister, asleep in our apartment above the store, suffocated from the smoke."

It had gotten so quiet that I could hear my own heart beating. "I'm one of your statistics, Shih," Jerry Cho said. "I watched my father burn to death and couldn't help him. I stood by while my sister suffocated. Police didn't do anything to the guys who set the fire, either. No evidence—"

Suddenly he pounded his fist on the pew in front of him and shouted, "Bad guys win in this society, good guys lose. We, the people, have to take power into our own hands and defend our rights."

"What you're talking about is vigilantism," Mr. Shih shot back, but people had begun to nod, to argue or agree with each other. As their voices rose, Rev. Thanh stepped hastily up to the podium.

"What we've heard tonight underscores the truth," he said in his beautiful, deep voice. "Now is the time for us of the AAG to stand together, to show publicly that the Asian community won't tolerate crimes against our brethren."

He was beginning to talk about organizing a march that would involve Asian groups statewide, when someone tugged at my hand. I looked down, surprised. I'd almost forgotten about Obaachan.

"Terri-chan," she whispered, "I feeling very hot. Must to go outside."

She really looked pretty pale. I told Mom what was going on, but, eyes glued to Rev. Thanh, she barely nodded as I led Obaachan past her and out of the church. Once out in the cool spring twilight, Obaachan sat down on a step, and I plumped down next to her.

"Are you okay?" I asked worriedly.

She nodded. "Okay now. Inside, too many people. Too much angriness is making me headache." She put a small hand to her forehead and closed her eyes.

Maybe I could get her some water? But as I got to my feet to find a cup and a water fountain, the church door opened again and Nick Kawalsky came out carrying a full paper cup. "I thought your grandmother might need this," he explained.

I asked how he could have read my mind, and he shrugged. "The church was pretty stuffy, and you and the old lady left together. I figured she might need some water." He pretended to pull at a pipe in his mouth. "Elementary process of reasoning, my dear Mizuno. It's what happens when you have a newspaperman for a dad."

63

Obaachan drank the water eagerly and thanked Nick in English and Japanese. As she was doing so, the door opened again and Jerry Cho came striding out with Damon at his heels. I couldn't hear what they were saying, but every movement Jerry made burned with rage.

That anger kindled my own fury, and I realized I was clenching my fists. I felt an almost irresistible need to go out and find Rodney Waring and hurt him, *destroy* him if I could. I hated him. *Hated him.*

Then something sour gurgled and frothed in my stomach, and I wanted to throw up. Obaachan was right. Too much anger was definitely making me sick.

FIVE

"DOESN'T SHE DO *anything* but criticize?" Alice complained.

I glanced at Obaachan's bent back, saw that she was out of hearing range, and shook my head. "Not if you happen to be female."

"Two minutes after I come through that door she's telling me I wear too much makeup and that my skirt is too short." Alice had caught a ride with a friend so that she could come home for the weekend to meet Obaachan, and already she'd had enough. "So I change into jeans and it's, 'Nice girl in Japan don't wear tight pants.' She's ten times worse than Dad."

Indignantly, Alice smoothed down her sleekly fitting designer jeans. "At least you get to bunk with Mitch. Try living in the same room with the old lady," I said. "Pick, pick, pick. 'Your mother never teach you how to hang up your clothes?' or, 'In Japan, only ragpicker wear pants with holes.' And then there's that spirit altar thing."

Obaachan had erected that altar two days after her arrival in Westriver. I'd come home from school on that day to find a *thing* on Alice's desk: an upended box on which sat photographs framed in black, a small incense burner (with burning incense in it), and plates of fruit, cakes, Japanese cigarettes, and car keys on a little silver dish.

The photographs were of our severe-looking Grandfather Mizuno, two very faded photos of old couples who had to be our great-grandparents on both sides,

65

and a smiling photo of Harris. Besides the photos were several stand-up wooden blocks with Japanese writing on them. Obaachan had told me these were the names of ancestors, and the names of her two babies who had died at birth.

"Each morning," I told Alice, "right after she gets out of bed, she bows to her altar and says good morning to it. Then she names everybody, including Harris. Whenever I hear her go 'Good morning, Harrisu,' it weirds me out."

Obaachan spent a lot of time before her spirit altar. Twice a day, in the morning, and in the evening, she knelt before it and chanted, *"Nanmyo horen gekkyo"* countless times. Occasionally she hit a small, bell-like thing with a little round stick.

"Why does she do that, anyway?" Alice asked me, now, and I said it had something to do with prayers for the dead. *"Shikataganai,"* Alice said, deadpan.

She was so tone perfect that I laughed out loud. Obaachan turned, saw us, and suggested in her whispery voice, "You girls help mother in kitchen."

Obaachan was, as usual, in black, but since this was a family gathering, she had put aside her black kimono in favor of a black sweater and straight black skirt that hung almost to her ankles. With that disapproving look in her narrow eyes, she looked like a lean, black crow.

As if aware of my thoughts, she gave us a critical look and asked, "Where Mitch-chan? I got cookie for him."

"Just the women get picked on," I reminded Alice as we headed for the kitchen. "Mitch-chan gets cookies, and Dad is a superior creature who has to be catered to."

"How's Mom taking it?" Alice grinned.

Mom was slamming around the kitchen. "And to think," she fumed, "that my own mother and father, may they rest in peace, raised me to think for myself. To know my own worth as a person and as a woman. They wanted me to follow my star. Now Mother Mizuno wants to keep me in the kitchen where she figures all females belong."

Alice and I nodded our sympathy. Mom stirred the gravy as if she hated it. "She can't even pronounce my name," she fumed, after a minute. I pointed out that Dad couldn't either, and she went, "That's different. He makes it sound—romantic."

Dad, *romantic*? I shook my head in disbelief. Alice struck a pose, rolled her eyes, and sighed, "Oh, Rora, Rora, wherefore art thou, Rora—instead of somebody with a name I can pronounce?"

Mom laughed, then swore as she burned herself. I watched her with pleasure. Having Alice home had brought a briskness to her movements and the old sparkle to her eyes.

"*Arré, arré*, why is noise? What is matter?" Obaachan made her slow way into the kitchen and peered doubtfully under each lid on the stove. "What you cook, Rora-san?"

"Roast chicken and rice with gravy, Mother Mizuno," Mom said, too heartily. "It's Alice's favorite dish."

Obaachan opened the oven door, snagged a fork, and prodded a bit of chicken loose. She tasted it and gave a nod of approval. "Chicken okay. Too bad American rice so dry—don't have good taste." She paused, choosing her next victim. "You study hard, A-ri-su?"

Alice said that she had a term paper to write and then finals. "You liking school?" Obaachan questioned.

"Sure, I do." Alice sounded bright and cheerful, but something in her voice made me look up at her.

"Is there a lot of talk about—about what happened?" Mom had caught the hesitation, too. When Alice reluctantly nodded, Mom asked, "What are people saying?"

"Most everybody says that Waring was totally wrong."

"And others believe he was just scared, that he's no

killer." Dad had come to stand in the kitchen doorway. "I hear it at work all the time," he added bitterly. "My son's murder has become common talk by the coffee machine."

"It's that woman's fault," Mom muttered.

She meant Grace Fallister, Waring's attorney. True to her reputation, Ms. Fallister had made sure that her client was always in the news, always in our face. The press loved her because she gave interviews left and right, dropped hints that the prosecution had no leg to stand on, and always insisted that her client was an innocent victim being railroaded by an ambitious prosecutor who had his heart set on becoming the next D.A.

"I heard on the news when we were driving down here that Fallister's hired a firm of trial consultants," Alice went on. "I guess their job is to try out every little angle that can get Waring off."

"It sucks," Mitch muttered. Mom turned away, biting her lip, and the lost, glazed look hovered in her eyes. I knew that she was seeing, as I was, the cruiser lights flaring against a wall of rain.

"God help me, I hate that man," she said in a low voice. "If he walked into the room now, I would try to kill him."

"You talk silly, Rora-san," Obaachan sounded shocked. "Must not to kill anybody."

"Sometimes, I'd like to," Dad said suddenly. His hands closed into tight fists as he repeated, "I'd like to."

In the silence that followed I noticed that our grandmother was watching Dad. Once she seemed about to speak but apparently changed her mind. No one said anything until Mom roused herself and told Mitch to wash his hands and asked Obaachan to come and sit down in the dining room.

"I'll take in the roast chicken," Mom said. "Will you carve it, Jun? Terri, you and Alice bring the vegetables." She still sounded stretched, still far away, and

I put my arm around her as she started to leave the kitchen. She tried to smile, but the warmth never reached her eyes.

Alice puffed out a long breath as the kitchen emptied. "It's the way things have been around here lately," I said. "I'm really worried about Mom. One minute she's okay, and the next she's in never-never land."

"I noticed. Well, it's not so great up at school, either." Eyes crinkled against the steam from the green beans, Alice added too casually, "Did I tell you Len and I broke up?"

It wasn't a total surprise. Alice hadn't mentioned Len Kamemoto once, even on the phone. Plus, I remembered how Len had shied away from her at the funeral.

"He just couldn't get past this shooting, you know?" Alice's voice trembled suddenly as she added, "He blames himself for what happened that night."

"But why? He couldn't have done anything to help Harris," I exclaimed. "Nobody blames him."

"Not out loud, maybe not even consciously. But Len said that whenever he saw Mom look at him, he knew she was wishing that he and Harris could have changed places."

Alice set down the beans and leaned back against the counter to look at me with uncharacteristically unhappy eyes. "He thinks it's his fault that his car broke down. He feels that he should have gone to Waring's house and not Harris."

"It's called survival guilt," I said. "I read an article about it one time for social studies. But, maybe it's not hopeless between you guys. I mean, you two were so much in love. Maybe if you give it time—"

"Len said that whenever he looked at me, he thought of Harris. He couldn't deal with that." Alice gave a little shrug and attempted her usual, flip tone. "So we agreed to go our separate ways. No biggie, Terriyaki. There's plenty more trout in the river."

But she was lying. Inside herself, in her own way, my sister was grieving. How many lives had Rodney Waring destroyed when he pulled the trigger? I thought of my own outpourings of hate and pain recorded in my journal upstairs.

"You know what?" Alice said softly. "I hate Rodney Waring worse than anyone. Mom's not the only one who thinks—I mean, sometimes I dream about choking him. I—I wouldn't blame Dad if he went and shot that creep."

"Me, neither. If Waring was dying right at my feet, and I could save him somehow, I'd spit in his face and watch him suffer."

We both stopped talking and stared into our own private vision of watching Waring die. Suddenly, the phone rang. Jolted back to reality I snapped up the receiver.

"Your brother got what he deserved," a raspy voice told me.

"Wh-who is this?" I stammered.

There was a chuckle on the other end of the wire. "You're gonna get yours, too, don't think you won't. Japs have taken away jobs from us white Americans long enough. Tell you what, girlie, if you slopes know what's best for you, you'll take the next boat home to Nippon. Or else, we'll—"

I slammed the receiver down, cutting him off. My heart was going a mile a minute, and I felt as if lice were crawling over my skin.

"Terri," Mom called from the other room, "who was it?"

"Nobody," I told her. "Wrong number."

I started to get the rice, but my hands shook so much I couldn't pick up the dish. Alice took it from me.

"Hate call?" she asked. Not looking at her, I nodded. "Yeah, well," she then said, "you'll get used to it, just try not to take it personally." I asked her what she meant by that and she went, "I mean, it's not only

70

you, Terriyaki. A few of those slimeballs have called me, too."

While we were still eating dinner, the phone recommenced ringing. *Not again*—I sat frozen in my seat as Dad took the call and came back to the table looking grim.

"Reverend Thanh thought we'd like to know that *New England Chronicle* is running a segment on our case. It airs in five minutes."

Silently, we left the table and filed into the den where we grouped ourselves on the couch. Obaachan arranged a cushion on the floor so she could kneel on it. Dad switched on the remote, and the two well-groomed program anchors, Carol Maldren and Jeffrey Shepherd, welcomed us to their program.

"Tonight's program deals with violence in New England," Carol Maldren began in her cool, competent voice. "Like everyone else, Jeffrey and I were horrified and saddened by what happened in Westriver on April nineteenth. A college-bound senior, an honor student, Harris Mizuno was shot and killed."

A gasp was wrenched from Mom as Harris suddenly smiled at us from the screen. I felt as if I'd dropped a thousand feet. No sound from Dad, but beside me on the floor Obaachan mumbled her prayers for the dead.

"We'd like to try and discover why our society is so plagued by suspicion and violence today," Jeffrey Shepherd interjected. "We've invited the noted criminologist, Dr. Paul Bayard, here to the studio tonight. Dr. Bayard will be with us shortly, but first Carol would like to take you behind the scenes of this tragedy."

Carol Maldren thanked her co-anchor and added that she'd recently visited Westriver. "*New England Chronicle* attempted to contact the Mizuno family but failed to do so," she said. I glanced at Dad's stony face and then turned my attention back to Ms. Maldren, who was adding that she respected our family's grief too much to pursue the matter.

"So tonight, we're going to explore another facet of the Mizuno shooting. We're going to learn more about Rodney Waring, who allegedly shot Harris Mizuno."

The cameras cut to Rodney Waring walking down the courthouse steps with his lawyer. "Grace Faris-ta," Obaachan murmured.

Grace Fallister was a big woman who carried herself as if she wanted to be even bigger. She wore a dark blue suit with a creamy white blouse, and neat pearl-and-gold earrings. She wasn't good looking, but her square-jawed face wasn't one you'd forget soon. Her gray-green eyes looked out of the TV right at you, judging and measuring your weaknesses so she'd know how and where to attack. Her voice was deep, as smooth as chocolate cream, as she said, "I have every confidence that justice will be served and that my client will be proved innocent of any crime."

The screen now shifted to Carol Maldren walking down the center of our town. This, Ms. Maldren said, was Westriver, where the Mizuno shooting occurred. This was where the alleged shooter, Rodney Waring, lived. She stopped and talked to a storekeeper, who said he'd known the Warings for years.

"I know him and his wife, the both of them. Don't believe for a moment Rodney's guilty of murder, either. It's not in him."

It wasn't true—the man was wrong. My heart skittered with adrenaline as Carol Maldren skillfully interviewed our town librarian, Waring's parish priest, and a neighbor, who swore that the Warings were good people.

"Last winter, when my wife got sick real sudden, Rod Waring drove her to the hospital. They've had a hard year, what with Jane having that hip-replacement surgery and then being beaten up by that purse snatcher."

The camera did a fade, and then closed in on a frail,

72

gray-haired woman sitting in a chair in a small, dark living room. She looked sad. "Rod was pretty shaken up by the attack," the neighbor's voice said, off camera. "Any right-thinking man would be."

Then, without warning, we were looking at Rodney Waring himself. Waring didn't look frail or troubled, as his neighbor had hinted. He looked healthy and solid. His hair was just graying at the temples, and under it he had a broad, ruddy face. His thick neck looked uncomfortable in shirt and tie.

Mitch swore. Dad commanded, "Be quiet."

Waring was speaking about his wife. "It's just me and Janey," he rumbled. "Just us two in the world. We was childhood sweethearts, goin' together since we was sixteen. Never had no kids. I don't know what I'd do without my Janey."

Mitch jumped up and ran out of the den, and I could hear his feet pounding up the stairs. I wanted to leave, too, but disgust and fascination kept me where I was while we returned to the studio. Here Jeffrey Shepherd spoke with his guest, Dr. Bayard, about rising crime statistics and how youth gangs were rampant. Senior citizens were, the criminologist assured us, *scared* of vicious young people.

"Traditionally," he added, "Americans have fought to keep their homes inviolate. Though the Mizuno shooting is a tragedy, we must also realize that Rodney Waring is also a victim of violence."

Carol Maldren now suggested that anyone who wanted to make a comment or ask a question could call the TV station. The first caller condemned violence in any form and said that it could have been her own son that Waring shot that rainy night. The second disagreed.

"I'm sorry that the Japanese boy died," he said, "but it's their fault in a way. If foreigners wouldn't come to America, taking jobs away from us Americans—"

Click. The TV screen went blank. Dad tossed down the remote, got up, went into the study, and shut the door. Mom sat there, making pleats in her skirt. "Those people didn't even know Harris," she whispered.

I couldn't bear the pain in her voice, so I got up, went to the phone, asked for information, and tapped out the station's number. Alice followed me. "You're calling the station?" she demanded, excitedly. "What're you going to say?"

Just then the line clicked and a female voice said, "*New England Chronicle.* May I ask your name and where you're calling from?"

"I'm calling from Westriver," I began. "My name is Terri Mizuno. I want to—"

"Please hold," the voice interrupted, and Muzak filled my ears. I stood there listening to elevator music and trying to quiet my jumping heartbeat, trying to formulate what I was going to say. *How dare you talk about my brother?* I'd say. *How dare you speak about justice while Waring walks free?*

Just then, I heard Carol Maldren's voice say, "We have a caller from Westriver on the line. There's reason to believe she's the shooting victim's sister. Hello, Terri Mizuno—you're on *New England Chronicle.*"

The shooting victim's sister. The words brought back that awful night so vividly that all the words I'd meant to say evaporated from my brain. "How can you?" I stammered into the phone. "You don't *know* him."

"Who are you calling, Terri?" Dad's voice made me jump. Literally. The phone receiver slipped out of my hand, and Dad caught it. He held it to his ear for a second, and then snapped it back into the cradle. Then he looked straight at me. "Why?" he demanded.

Transfixed by his frown, I stammered, "I wanted to tell them how wrong they are."

"How would you have gone about doing that? They're professionals, Terri. They'd have made you look foolish in a second." Dad's frown deepened. "Don't you ever think before you act?"

74

Behind me, Alice protested indignantly, "Terri's just mad because of that program. Aren't you angry, too?"

"Of course I am. But I won't allow our family's grief to be turned into a media circus. That's why I refused to have any part of this program when the TV people called." Dad eyed me sternly. "Next time," he said, "*think*."

Humiliated, feeling like ten kinds of fool, I headed for the kitchen where I started to wash the dishes. Alice joined me. As we worked in silence, all the things I'd wanted to say to the *New England Chronicle* anchor and the so-called criminologist came foaming into my mind.

So I stayed awake late that night, writing. Because Obaachan went to bed early, I ended up in the bathroom. Perched on the john, I kept on writing until my fingers numbed and my head ached, till my rear end actually cramped from sitting on the hard toilet cover. When the gush of words finally slowed down, it was three in the morning.

I went to school next day with less than four hours of sleep and found Nick Kawalsky waiting for me. "You weren't at the biology field trip Friday," he said. "I took notes for you."

I told him thanks, explained that I'd missed the field trip because Alice had come home on Friday morning, and I'd wanted to be there. "Anything happen?" I asked, without much interest.

"Teddy Peerse and her boyfriend wandered off and later found that they'd been making out in a patch of poison ivy." I winced. "George Elder got into trouble for pushing Hy Fallon into the water. Me, I collected my water samples and studied tide pools. I also found this."

He thrust his hand into his pocket and brought out a blue shell. It was small, snail-like, and glowed in Nick's palm like a piece of sky. "Here," he said casually, "you can keep it if you like."

Then he changed the subject. "What did you think of that so-called criminologist they had on *New England Chronicle* last night?"

I said that the man was a class-A jerk. "I know you called the station," Nick continued. "How come you didn't stay on the line?"

Not wanting to get into what had happened with Dad, I explained that I'd been so mad that I was speechless. "Later on, I thought of everything I'd have liked to say," I added.

Kawalsky just nodded, and I felt the tense muscles of my neck ease a little. The nice thing about Nick was that I could say exactly what was on my mind, and he understood. "I did spend hours writing in my journal," I admitted.

"So instead of calling the station, write what you feel," he suggested. "Write a letter to the editor of the *Herald*. You could use your journal as reference."

I told him that what I wrote in my journal was private and would stay that way. "I'm not about to spill my guts to the world," I added.

"When you called last night, you said that they didn't know Harris," Nick argued. "*Tell* them." I started walking toward my homeroom, but he followed me. "I brought something to show you," he said. "Read it when you're alone."

Without further comment he handed me a notebook. There was no doubt as to what this was. "Why do you want me to read *your* journal?" I asked.

Nick got a little pink over his bony cheekbones where, I now noted, a few freckles floated aimlessly. "You'll see," he said. Then he waved, hefted his book bag, and headed up the corridor to his own homeroom. Bewildered, I watched him go until a familiar voice spoke at my shoulder.

"So you've got that skinny wuss taking notes for you, huh?"

Damon had come up so softly I hadn't even heard his approach. He was standing so close to me that I could smell the mellow tang of his after-shave. "How've you been, Terri?" he asked.

What was it about Damon Ying that made my already scanty power of speech totally dry up? It took an effort just to reply that I was fine. After this fascinating and intelligent reply, I kicked myself and, as usual, thought of things I *could* have said.

"You look good," he then said. "You're always quiet and pretty—like a tall green bamboo." Was he talking about *me*? "My old lady has this Chinese scroll painting with a bamboo on it," Damon went on. "It makes me think of you."

I stammered, oh, sure, I was as *skinny* as a bamboo. Then, remembering how Len Kamemoto had compared Alice to a chrysanthemum, I kicked myself for my heavy-footed attempt at humor.

Terri, you are such a derf—but Damon just laughed. "Forget it. I should've said, you remind me of Harris."

"Of *Harris*?" This time I was shocked out of being nervous. "But we're—we were nothing like each other. Harris did everything right. He's—he *was* so smart and quick and everybody looked up to him—"

My throat closed up in a knot the size of a fist, my eyes stung. As I blinked them clear of mist, I heard Damon say, "Yeah, but with Harris, you never had to pretend. All you had to be was yourself, and that was okay with him."

I thought of Harris's army of friends. "He was like that," I agreed.

Someone in the near distance was shouting Damon's name. He started to walk away, then reached out and touched my shoulder. "Terri," he said, "I know it's rough on you, but you're not alone, okay? If something or somebody bothers you, you let me know. I mean it, pretty girl."

I was so shaken that I actually dropped Kawalsky's journal. Hastily kneeling down to pick it up, I saw that the notebook had flipped open to a page with

77

three-inch-high words on it. "MOM WAS MUR-DERED," the words told me.

Each of those words speared me like a knife. I could feel the hatred burning in them as well as Nick's unbearable pain. I didn't need to read this—I had problems of my own.

But instead of closing the journal, I flipped a few pages forward to where Nick had written: "Reasons why I miss Mom."

In his usual, reasonable way, Nick proceeded to catalog those reasons. Then he progressed to his feelings. When he wrote about hearing a voice that sounded like hers in a crowd and whipping around to look, because *maybe* it was a dream and his mom was really alive, my eyes brimmed over with tears. Because wasn't that the way I felt about Harris? Hadn't I searched for him in crowds, in my dreams, in my mind?

Now I knew why Nick had brought the journal to show me. He'd wanted me to know I wasn't the only one who'd walked down this road. And if that were true, if there were other people out there who'd felt as Nick and I did, they might be able to see Harris the way I did, get to know him, *feel* his death. And if they could do that they might see just how much damage Waring had done that rainy night—

"Get out of my way!" someone snapped, behind me.

Before I could move, I was roughly shouldered aside, and two guys swaggered past—a chunky, square-faced boy with close-cropped, rusty-colored hair—Link Lewis. The zit-faced, towheaded senior with him was one of his buddies.

"This damn school is full of slopes," Link Lewis said loudly, and his sleazy sidekick snickered. "Just keep out of my way, slant eyes, or—"

His taunt turned into a yelp of surprise as Damon Ying came up behind him and kicked him behind the knee. Link went flying forward onto his knees. "Oops—I tripped," Damon Ying said.

Link's sidekick shouted a curse and charged Damon, who hip checked him, and then flipped him to the floor. "Tripped again," he laughed.

"Fight," somebody shouted, "fight!"

Homerooms emptied into the corridor and a few guys, probably friends of the brain-dead duo, tore into Damon. But Damon had a lot of friends, too. Guys from the football team, loyal fans, and even some girls rushed into battle.

Involuntarily I started forward, but someone grabbed my arm and hauled me back. "Are you crazy, or what?" Kawalsky yelled in my ear.

A half-dozen teachers led by Mr. Bandy, the football coach, had come running down the hall. Mr. Bandy grabbed Damon with one hamlike hand and the other guy with the other and roared, "I said, break this *up!*"

Nick started dragging me down the corridor. "Let's get *out* of here," he said.

"But, Damon—"

"Damon's having a good time. He started it, remember?"

"He didn't start anything," I protested. "Link was in my face, and he was standing up for me."

" 'An eye for an eye makes the world blind,' " Nick retorted.

"Mahatma Gandhi," I said automatically.

"He was right. Trouble is, guys like Damon think all there is to life is good guys beating up bad guys. Superhero stuff."

Indignant at Nick's lofty tone I cried, "So where were *you*, huh? I didn't see you doing anything to stop the fight, Mr. Bigmouth."

"What, *me* against lobotomized Link and his sidekick?" Nick looked shocked. "They'd have had me for breakfast. When I heard them start, I ran into the next room and called down to the office to get Mr. Bandy."

But Kawalsky's logic didn't convince me one bit. I was thinking of Waring again and wishing that I could get him alone so I could hit him and hit him, as Damon had hit Link just now. And maybe, if I hit hard enough, the gnawing pain inside me would go away.

SIX

MISSING THAT BIOLOGY field trip ended up being a royal pain. I had to do an assignment based solely on Nick's notes, and because it wasn't good enough for Ms. Corcoran, she made me stay after school, Thursday, and do it over.

I took the late bus home and was halfway down the driveway when I heard Mitch's excited voice. "But, Obaachan," my brother was crying, "he just wants to be friendly."

Agitated squawks followed, mostly in Japanese. Wondering what Mitch was doing to get Obaachan so riled up, I jogged the rest of the driveway and opened the door just as Obaachan cried, "Mitch-chan, damé, damé, you cannot do such a things!"

There in the hall area was my kid brother. Plopped at his feet was a dirty, flop-eared, black-and-tan mutt that looked to be a cross between a Saint Bernard and a dust mop.

"Don't tell me," I said. "He followed you home."

Mitch ignored my sarcasm. "Well, yeah, he did, sort of. I found him on the road home from school," he said defensively. "Poor guy must've been abandoned or something. Look at his paws."

He knelt down and took one of the dog's paws, and the animal flopped down, belly up, and waved all four feet in the air. He wasn't quite grown but not a pup, either, skinny under all that matted hair. And his gray pads were scuffed and bleeding. It made me ache to look at those hurt paws, because I knew how long the dog must've trudged for them to get that way.

"Poor guy." Mitch was watching my face and knew I was a convert. "I couldn't just leave him out there, abandoned, could I, Terr? Huh, Terr?"

Terr. Harris had always called me that. Now the ache in my midsection had nothing to do with my little brother's flea-bitten friend.

Obaachan grabbed my shoulder and tried tugging me away. "Don't touch, dog is dirty," she scolded. "Have fleas! Have *dani.* Not can bring in house. Father be so mad. Maybe we get sick from dog."

"What's *dani*?" Mitch asked. I shrugged. "Don't worry, Obaachan, he's got his shots. See?"

The animal had his rabies vaccination tag tied to a rope around his neck. "I'm gonna call him Walker, on account of he walked all this way," Mitch said happily. Walker licked Mitch's cheek. He then licked my hands and feet. He tried to do the same for Obaachan, but she retreated up the stairs, muttering in Japanese.

"Dog is too big, too dirty," she reiterated. "No bring in house."

For once, Mom agreed with her mother-in-law. "That beast is crawling with every varmint on this earth," she exclaimed when she got home later that afternoon. "No way are you keeping him. No." She added sternly as Mitch opened his mouth, "All we need is a huge, Heinz-57 creature around here, and don't give me any of that 'aw, Ma,' stuff, either. Don't you know I have allergies?"

She stopped talking, sneezed three times in rapid succession, and added in a nasal voice, "I'm calling the shelter."

"I'll wash him. I'll feed him. I'll build him a doghouse outside next to the rabbit hutch. *Puh-leeze,* don't call the shelter, Ma," Mitch implored. "They'll just kill him there."

I said, maybe if I shopped around, I could help find another home for Walker. Mom kept on sneezing, and

82

Obaachan observed that no *properly* brought up Japanese child argued with his elders. Walker, as if he knew his fate was hanging by a thread, howled like a banshee.

"Uh—hi," a diffident voice said from the doorway. I turned to see Nick Kawalsky's head poking halfway through. "I—ah, came to give you this." Then he did a half-wave thing and added hastily, "Later."

Obaachan said, now, see what has happened—we have embarrassed ourselves in front of a guest. I picked up the paper that Nick had tossed on the hall table. It was open to the editorial page.

And there was my letter to the editor, the one I'd handed Nick this Tuesday. I'd been waiting to hear what Mr. Kawalsky had to say about it, and when I hadn't heard, figured he'd dumped it in file thirteen. I surely hadn't expected to see it in print.

It was embarrassing and scary and exciting at the same time. Not wanting to stand there and read the thing in front of my still-arguing family, I went outside and shut the door after me.

Kawalsky was just climbing up on his bicycle, but now he paused. "So what do you think?" he asked. I shook my head, plopped down on the porch stairs, and commenced to read what I'd written, wincing as a dumb word hit me here and there and because I'd used "terrible" three times in one paragraph.

"What's the matter with you? It's a good letter," Kawalsky protested as I groaned out loud. He was leaning on the handlebars of his bike, watching me. "Dad said that he was touched, that he really got to know Harris. That's what you wanted, right?"

I was about to tell Nick that I wasn't so sure if I should've ever written this letter much less had it published when the front door opened, and Obaachan peered out. "Terri-chan," she hissed, "bring friend inside. I make tea."

Kawalsky looked surprised. I told Obaachan that he probably had things to do, but he said, "Sure—why

83

not. Thanks, ma'am. Now you can show your family the paper, Terri."

I'd definitely have chosen another time—*much* later—and glared at Nick when Obaachan wanted to know, what paper? Ignoring my evil looks, Nick explained.

Naturally everybody read the darn thing. So what do you do while everybody in your family is clustered around reading something you wrote? I felt so nervous that I wanted to find a hole and climb down into it. I glared at Kawalsky, who smiled back at me in an irritating way.

"*You* write this?" Eyes round, Obaachan stared at me as if I'd grown two heads. "I cannot believe."

"I told you that Terri is *smart*, Mother Mizuno," Mom was smiling, but her eyes were wet. "This is a beautifully written letter. It—it reaches the heart. How did you find the right words, honey?"

I shrugged, not having *any* words, right now, to describe what I'd felt. It was weird how different I'd felt while I was writing the letter. Then, it was as if my thoughts had changed into music that sang the song of Harris's life.

"Your father will be so proud of you, Terri," Mom was saying. Then she added, "I wonder if Mr. Shih has read this? We must send him a copy."

Nick promised to get extra copies, and I belatedly introduced him. Mom said, "We met at the AAG meeting, didn't we? I've read and enjoyed your father's editorials, Nick. He's a man of integrity."

Obaachan, her sense of hospitality returning, served up an honorable three o'clock. Meanwhile, Mitch strategically took Walker outside and made a run for him near the rabbit hutch. By the time Mom remembered about the dog it was late, and she was too preoccupied with my letter to think about calling the shelter.

"He can stay in the backyard overnight," she told

my beaming brother, "but tomorrow, unless you can come up with another home for him, he's out of here."

Elated, Mitch whistled himself outside to feed Walker and the bunnies, and Obaachan said she needed my help cutting vegetables for dinner. It was, she told me, not good enough that I wrote letters to the paper. I needed to be introduced to so-called womanly skills.

"Cut more small, more small," she carped at me. "You have such rough hand for cutting vegetable, Terri-chan. Not get husband in Japan with rough hand like that. When my granddaughter Kazu-chan was your age, she cut more better than you."

If Obaachan terrorized her granddaughter the way she did us, she was probably having a party in her absence. About to say that I had no wish for a husband, Japanese or otherwise, I suddenly got this vivid mental flash of Damon Ying.

Damon swooping down on Link Lewis like an avenging angel, Damon telling me I reminded him of a tall, graceful bamboo— "Tell me about my Japanese cousins," I said hastily.

Obaachan talked about the boys first (naturally), bragging about what bright students they were and how hard they studied. "They go *juku* school all time," she said proudly. "From time they are five. Every day after school, *juku*."

Apparently this *juku* was some kind of prep school that helped kids in Japan compete with other kids. "Must study to enter good university," Obaachan said smugly.

"You mean they have to begin studying when they're *five*?"

"Have to start sometime." Obaachan shifted gears and went into her criticism mode. "Bad education in America," she said. "Mamas should make sure chirrun study. My daughter—she always busy driving chirrun around from *juku*."

And Mom had often complained about driving us

kids to sports practices and clubs. I thought of my cousins being chauffeured from school to school while still in kindergarten. It blew my mind. "I like our system better here in America," I said.

Obaachan leveled a keen look at me. "In America," she said sternly, "chirrun take gun and knife to school." I began to protest that things like this didn't happen at Westriver Junior-Senior High, and she said, "In Japan, nobody get shot for knocking on stranger's door."

The words I'd meant to say shriveled up and died within me. Obaachan started to chop again. "Why you don't study more? You disappoint you papa."

"I do study. Dad just doesn't think I measure up whatever I do."

Obaachan looked puzzled. "I mean I'm not smart, like Harris was," I explained, "and I'm not pretty, like Alice, or the baby of the family, like Mitch. When I try to talk to people, my tongue ties up in knots. When I do something, it usually turns out wrong. *Ta-daa!* Here I am, your average, everyday, tongue-tied klutz."

In proof of which I spread my arms, knocking the cutting board to the floor. I thought Obaachan would get after me for that, but to my surprise, she just picked up the board and said, "Don't matter, Terri-chan. After he see newspaper, you papa proud."

I'd planned to take my time showing Dad that newspaper, to casually explain about my letter to the editor, but Mitch spoiled my plan. The minute Dad got into the house he bounced up to him and waved the *Westriver Herald* under his nose. "Look at what Terri did," he shouted.

"Don't yell," Dad said automatically. His eyebrows pulled together as he glanced at the editorial page, and the tightness became a frown as he read. "He hates it," I said. Almost, but not quite, joking.

"Of course not," Dad said impatiently. "That's a foolish thing to say." He read the letter again and then said, "Well." Well, *what*? "It isn't a bad letter, Terri,

86

but you should have discussed it with me first. And as I told you the other night, many things you say here are private to the family."

"It shows what kind of a man Harris was," Mom said, bristling to the defense. "What he meant to us and to the community. That's exactly what Kurt Shih said we should do, and I think Terri did a terrific job."

"What do you want me to say? I told you, it's not bad."

Dad put the paper down on the table and walking toward the stairs asked when dinner would be ready. I stood there feeling as if I'd dived into what I thought was a sparkly pool and found out it was a mud puddle.

During dinner, Dad didn't mention my letter even once. He talked instead about a meeting he'd had with his boss that morning about being transferred to another department. He wasn't happy about it. "Winchell called it a promotion," he said, "but I get the feeling that my being the customer-service manager is an embarrassment for ROTA right now. There's been too much publicity about the trial, and they want me less visible."

I left the folks talking and did the dishes with Mitch. I told myself that I hadn't expected any praise from Dad, but my feelings stayed hurt. Well, not really hurt, but—bruised. After all, if Mr. Kawalsky had printed the letter, it couldn't have been so bad.

To even out my bumpy feelings, I went with my kid brother when he took Walker for a run that evening. It was a warm May evening and windows were open, and on the way home, we heard a popular radio talk-show host declaring that the Mizuno shooting was a by-product of the immigrant invasion of America.

"What we need to do is to restrict immigration to white Anglo-Saxons," the talk-show host was saying in a pleasant, reasonable voice. "Then our own people's jobs would be secure, and the violence on our streets would lessen. I've never been in favor of what people like Harvey Silcom stand for, but I'm beginning to understand why white supremacist groups are becoming so popular."

"Terri?"

Melanie Reed had come out of her house and was standing across the street from us. "Is he yours?" Mel continued. "I thought your mom's allergic to dogs."

"He's staying with us for a while," I said. I didn't want to talk to Mel. So, with the talk-show host's mellow, bigoted voice still following us, Mitch and I started walking away.

Mel crossed the street and came after us. "You don't have to talk to her," Mitch said to me loudly.

Melanie pretended she didn't hear him. "I read your letter in the paper," she told me. "It made me cry." Her voice shook. "I—I'm really so sorry, Terri."

Since our confrontation, I'd hated Mel as a traitor. Now, hearing the sadness in her voice, I felt miserable and unsure. I stayed quiet while she went on, "I just wanted to tell you—I think of what happened that awful night all the time. I liked Harris a lot, and I'm miserable that he died."

Isn't that enough? Melanie's voice pleaded with me, and the tremble in it reminded me how Mel had been the first person at school who'd been friendly to me. I thought of how close we'd become, of all the times we'd slept over at each other's houses and whispered secrets about cute boys in the dark. I remembered the triumphs we'd shared, the disasters over which we'd consoled each other.

But all of that belonged to another reality. Now, everything hinged on one thing. "Do you still think Waring's not a murderer?" I demanded.

Reluctantly, she nodded. I turned away from her, knowing I had nothing more to say to Mel, now or ever. *Those who aren't for us are against us*, I could hear Damon saying, and hate for Waring sucked me down like quicksand. He'd taken both Harris and Melanie away from me.

In silence, Mitch and I walked up to our house just as Mom came hurrying out, calling my name. For a second, my heart quit working—something awful had to have happened—and then I saw that Mom's eyes were shining.

"The *Boston Globe* just called. It wants to publish your letter on its editorial page," she exclaimed. Almost babbling with pleasure, she dragged me into the house. "Imagine, Terri—your letter's good enough to reprint in the *Globe!*"

As I stared at her in total disbelief, the study door opened and Dad looked out. "The *Boston Globe* wants to publish *Terri's* letter?" he demanded.

Mom nodded. "What do you say about your daughter now, Jun Mizuno?"

My father looked thoughtful. "We'll have to ask Kurt Shih if it's okay," he cautioned. "The *Herald* is just a local paper, but the *Boston Globe* has a huge circulation. Maybe it can jeopardize the trial." He glanced at me, cleared his throat. "I'm sure you understand the need for precaution, Terri. I'll phone Mr. Shih in the morning."

"Jun!" Mom exclaimed indignantly. "Is that all you can say? Terri writes a wonderful letter that a major newspaper wants to print, and all you can think of is Kurt Shih's reaction?"

Dad actually looked uncomfortable. "What do you want me to say?" he countered. Then he quickly shut the study door.

There was a little silence. Mom exclaimed, "Inside, he's glowing with pride, but he can't express it. He's doing what you kids call the Japanese Thing."

"Not good show pride over what chirrun do," Obaachan added her two cents. "Show too much pride. Pride is punish by bad luck."

But I knew that wasn't so. When Dad had been proud of something Harris did—or of something Alice or Mitch did—his eyes shone, and even though he did the Japanese Thing, you *knew* he was jumping for joy inside. Tonight I wasn't at all sure that there'd been pleasure in his eyes.

So, I asked myself, what else was new? Some things never change. I was—would always be—the gawky, awkward-tongued, unsatisfactory daughter, the one who always could be counted on to do the wrong thing.

I was too heavy hearted even to write in my journal that night, and it took awhile to fall asleep. When I finally drifted under, I dreamed that Harris and Mitch and me were running in the backyard and that suddenly Mitch's bunnies had grown as big as horses and were having a race with Walker, who was making a lot of noise barking and howling as he dashed around the house.

Bark, bark, bark—

I awoke, heart pounding, for I realized this was no dream. There were sounds, too—rustling sounds right under my window. Walker was barking himself into a fit.

Those weren't bunnies out there. I jumped out of bed and ran to the window, jerked back as I saw shadows dotting our front yard. Then there was this splintering, crashing sound, and I screamed as something came hurtling through the window.

It landed on my bed. Oh, Lord—a bomb! "Obaachan," I yelled, "wake up, get *down!*"

I grabbed her by the arm, pulled her to the floor, dragged her behind my bed just as another window splintered. Accompanied by spewed fragments of glass, something heavy bumped down on the floor at our feet.

A brick—at least, it wasn't a bomb. But Obaachan fell flat on the floor shrieking, "*Senso! Is the war!*"

She began muttering her prayers over and over under her breath. "*Namyo horen gekkyo—*" Another splintering crash, and Mom's voice shouting to know if we were all right.

"Terri?" Mom shouted. "Terri, answer me! Are you

90

hurt?" She came running in, Mitch right behind her, and put her arms around me, hands and eyes checking me out to see if I was okay.

"Slopeheads," I heard a man's gravelly voice bellow, 'you ain't wanted here." There was a flare of light and I thought—supposing they burn the house down?

Then there were sirens in the distance. "The police are coming—it's okay," I whispered to Obaachan, who was praying louder now. Mom asked, was she all right? "Yes, yes," Obaachan quavered. "Not hurt. Where is Juntaro?"

We found him downstairs staring at the wreck of our living room. Light bounced over a thousand shards of glass, and a brick, deformed from years in the ground, lay in the center of the carpet.

"Nowhere to be found," Dad replied to Mom's terrified question. "I have no idea where they went—the bastards."

His face was very red, his hands clenched in a rage I'd never seen before. "I could kill them all," he muttered. "See what they've done."

He dragged Mom outside and Mitch ran after them. With Obaachan clinging to my arm, I followed. There, lit in the red and blue revolving lights I saw that the front of our house had been spray painted with black paint.

The huge black words proclaimed, "WARING SHOULD HAVE SHOT YOU, TOO."

Bad news, Mom always said, runs fast. Next morning at the bus stop, all the kids gathered around Mitch and me to ask questions. Melanie hung back, but her eyes asked the question on everyone else's lips: "Do you know who did it?"

Damon caught up to me before homeroom. Instead of asking me "The Question," he went, "That was a good letter you wrote to the *Herald*."

I thanked him and he stood there balancing his books in the crook of one smooth, golden arm and

91

rocking lightly on the balls of his feet like a jungle cat about to spring.

"I know who paid you a visit last night," he said, after a minute. "Jerry's pretty sure that those bozos belonged to the Brotherhood of SAW, the Society of Aryan Warriors. It's a local hate group."

I'd never heard of the Brotherhood of SAW before. "How does Jerry know?" I asked, and Damon said that his cousin had his sources.

"Did you know he founded the Asian Power through Unity group in L.A.?" he asked proudly. "The APU stood up to creeps who tried to push Asians around, creeps like this hate group here, and it worked. *Nobody* crosses Jerry."

I asked why Jerry had left California. "There was some kind of hassle," Damon explained offhandedly. "APU members got a bit rough with a guy who they knew had burned down a Korean grocery store. The cops—what's new?—sided with the criminals."

He paused. "I told Jerry he should start an APU group here in Westriver, and he's thinking about it. We need leadership, especially if the SAW starts acting up."

"Mr. Shih says—" I began.

He cut me off. "You won't get diddly from him, Terri. The man's a pol. Shih doesn't care a damn about Harris. Only reason he's charging Waring with murder two and not manslaughter is so's he can get enough publicity out of the trial to be elected D.A."

Damon's words kept surfacing throughout the day because everybody I met in class or in the corridor during passing or at lunch or in gym knew about what had happened to us. Everybody had an opinion. The kids and teachers who agreed with me said that what had happened was totally disgusting, immoral, and unconscionable, and that the police should find the creeps and punish them to the full extent of the law.

But there were the others. They didn't come up to

ne and snicker, "Hey, I'm a racist." Instead, they
stood in the halls and watched me, whispering to each
other. And, during lunch when I went to sit at my
usual place, I found a huge smear of ketchup on the
seat forming the word *gook*.

I was calmer than the kids I was with. While they
freaked and ran to get the lunch monitor, I got paper
towels and wiped off the mess. But later, when I
found a hate note jammed inside my book bag, I almost lost it. The note said: "Your days are numbered,
Jap. The Brotherhood of SAW will get you." It was
decorated with a white fist holding an upraised
sword.

I tore up the note and threw it away, but the memory of it clung like a foul odor. I spent sixth period
looking around at the kids in my class, wondering if
one of *them* had written that sick note, or if Link
Lewis himself had somehow snuck up close enough to
me to shove the note into my book bag.

By the end of school, I'd had it with looking at faces
and suspecting each one. I was in such a terrible
mood that I was actually glad that I had to stay after
school and make up an English quiz.

In fact I purposely missed the late bus so that I
could be alone. Hefting my book bag, I was heading
down School Road to South Street when I heard a
whir of bicycle wheels behind me and Nick Kawalsky
rode up.

"You looked ready to inflict serious bodily harm on
somebody," he said. I growled, he had better believe it.
"Bad day, huh? How about cooling down with an ice
cream?" He then added, "I'm buying."

I thought it over, nodded, and climbed up behind
Nick on his bike. As we rode to South Street, I asked
why he was headed downtown in the first place. "Dad
gave me a couple of things to mail at the post office,"
he said. "It'll just take a minute, and—lookit—there's
Lewis. What's he doing?"

I peered over his shoulder and saw Link standing

near the library steps handing out what looked to be flyers to passers-by. Beside him was a broad-shouldered, chunky guy in a camouflage uniform. His hair was closely cropped, and for a second I thought he was a marine. Then he looked toward us, and I saw my mistake.

The badge he wore on his chest was no military insignia. It was the now-familiar emblem of the fist and the sword. And though he wore dark glasses behind which his eyes were invisible, I still could feel the impact of this man's hate and contempt.

"Let's get out of here," I muttered.

Instead of listening to me, Kawalsky stopped pedaling, bent, and scooped up one of the leaflets that someone had dropped. "What a bunch of crap," he exclaimed.

He passed the leaflet to me. In neatly scripted words the leaflet informed me that the northeast coast of America was in danger of being destroyed by racially inferior lowlifes and that whites had to fight to regain their homeland.

" 'America is meant for the white race—beast-men should go back to Africa and Asia—' " That was as far as I got before Nick snatched the paper out of my hands.

"Listen to this: 'Our brave warriors are ready to reclaim our white heritage. We, the Society of Aryan Warriors, ally ourselves with our brothers of the SAW. Our weapons are ready for a war of liberation.' Crap!"

He scrunched up the paper and furiously threw it on the ground. "Nobody in his right mind's going to believe this garbage."

But as he spoke I watched Link handing a leaflet to a nice-looking woman about Mom's age. She glanced down at it, folded it, and put it in her purse. She didn't act repulsed in any way.

"They've come because of Waring," I muttered. "They're here to help him."

"Like flies to a road kill," Nick agreed. The disgust

his voice deepened. "Well, Link finally found a group dumb enough for him to belong to. Look at him o at it."

Suddenly, anger boiled up in me. Without bothering o think, I hopped off Nick's bicycle and started walking toward Link Lewis.

He was too busy handing out his fliers to notice me. I got right in front of him, so close that I could see that he was wearing the same badge his friend was sporting. Not looking at me, Link handed me a paper, and I said, "Thanks, for nothing."

I tore the flyer in two. Then I tore it in four. Link stared at me in bug-eyed surprise as I snarled, "That's what I think of you and your so-called brotherhood."

"Way to go, Terri." Kawalsky had caught up to me. He added, "I knew you were brain damaged, Lewis, but I didn't know how bad till now."

Link Lewis had turned crimson. He was so mad, he stuttered. "You g-get out of my face!"

At that moment, the chunky skinhead turned toward us. "Trouble, bro?" he drawled.

Link started to stutter even harder saying that I was giving him a hard time. "And her d-daddy's a fat cat at ROTA, took a raise when m-my pop got canned," he whined. "Fat cat, taking jobs from white Americans—"

"The mongreloids always do." The older guy sneered. "What's wrong with you, boy?" he then asked Nick. "Can't get no white girl to go with you?"

"You watch your mouth," Kawalsky snapped.

"Or what, junior?"

The skinhead whipped off his glasses. Strange eyes—one blue, one brown, stared at us with reptilian coldness, and I suddenly realized what an idiotic thing I was doing. The skinhead might have a gun, or a knife—something I hadn't thought of till now because I was so mad. Now, as though he'd read my mind, the proud Aryan warrior raised his right hand,

95

mimicked a pistol, and pantomimed shooting us both dead.

I put a hand on Nick's arm. "Leave it," I whispered. "They're not worth it. Let's just get out of here."

As we walked away, we could hear Link and the skinhead laughing.

SEVEN

WAS DOING homework in my room when Mitch came
barreling in. He snatched off my Walkman headset,
which I wore so I wouldn't have to listen to Obaachan
chanting her prayers, and shouted, "Terri, come on
down. They're talking about our case on TV."

"Again?" A nervous spasm kicked around in my
stomach as I followed Mitch down to the den where a
TV newsbreak special was reporting the meeting between Harvey Silcom, the supreme leader of the Society of Aryan Warriors, and Rodney Waring.

Television cameras now showed a blond-haired guy
in an expensive-looking gray suit shaking hands with
Waring. "Your friends are all behind you, Rodney,"
Harvey Silcom said in a pleasant, soft-spoken drawl.
"Our brothers and sisters are out on the street now,
making sure that the good people of this town know
about the injustice that's been done to you."

Apparently this Harvey Silcom headed up a white-
supremacist organization headquartered in Louisiana. He came across as handsome, well educated, and
very, very slick. "He's dangerous," Mitch muttered.
"People are going to believe him."

Silcom, the news reporter informed us, was in New
England with some of his top-ranking aides to address a gathering of the Brotherhood of SAW. "The
SAW are a local branch of the Society of Aryan Warriors," he explained. "Several members of the SAW
were seen in Westriver, where Harris Mizuno was
shot and killed in April."

There was a quick cut to skinheads in camouflag
uniforms handing out leaflets on South Street, an
then a fade to Westriver's somber-eyed Police Chie
Jordan, who said that no white supremacist grou
national or local, was going to cause violence i
Westriver—

Click. The screen went dead. "All they do is talk,
Dad said grimly. "Nothing ever comes of it."

Mitch said, "I wish I could *get* that Harvey Silcom.
He pointed his finger at the now dead TV screen
"*Kapow!*" he shouted. "That's what I'd like to do!"

Dad, who'd been heading toward his study, stoppe
dead in his tracks. "I never want to hear you say tha
again," he told Mitch.

"But, D-Dad!" My kid brother was so indignant tha
he could hardly talk. "That jerk and all his friends ar
out to hurt us. And—and anyway, when Damon an
his cousin jumped those skinheads, you wanted to joi
them."

Our father said that had been different, a matter o
honor. "A man may fight with his fists to avenge a
insult," he added sternly, "but I won't have any tal
about violence from you or anyone else. It doesn'
solve anything."

"It gets things done," Mitch muttered, but he said i
after Dad had disappeared into his study.

Next morning, the papers carried a full account o
the supremacist leader and his local hate-grou
branch. "I wish someone'd *do* something," Mitch
growled as we headed for school. "I feel like I'm just
sitting here waiting for those creeps to attack me o
something."

We'd reached the end of our driveway as he spoke,
and from there we could both see Mrs. Despard standing in the Blankards' yard, talking to Emily. "Look at
that," my brother exclaimed. "I thought Emily
couldn't stand that woman. Let's get out of here before they see us."

We quickened our step. As we passed, I overheard

Mrs. Despard saying, "It *used* to be a nice, safe neighborhood. Now, you can't even be secure in your own house. I tell you, I couldn't sleep a wink for the past few nights. Who knows if they'll get the right house next time?"

The right house. Mrs. Despard didn't care two beans about us—she was just worried that the so-called Brotherhood of SAW would make a mistake and throw a brick through *her* window.

And Emily Blankard, supposedly our friend, was standing there listening and nodding. The day suddenly seemed to turn colder and, as we walked down Ferndale Street, shaded by trees now green with the darling buds of May, I felt as if eyes were watching us. Eyes from windows and from behind doors, from backyards and cars parked in driveways—all of them wondering what we would do next. And not all those eyes were friendly.

This was all Rodney Waring's fault. Bricks being heaved through our windows, hate groups having a field day in Westriver, and neighbors and friends turning on us—all of this had started with the action of one man.

And he was still free, still not imprisoned for his crimes. While the judge took his time setting a date for the trial and Ms. Fallister kept publicity for Waring simmering, while the Brotherhood of SAW grew bold in the support of Harvey Silcom's hateful white supremacists, the velvet-faced Swiss pansies Mom had planted on Harris's grave bloomed and faded and bloomed again.

I got to know those flowers well. Each Sunday, Mom, Obaachan, Mitch, and I drove out to Silverbirch Cemetery to water the flowers. Dad never came with us, and Mom said he liked to go to the cemetery alone.

One time I picked a flower—a huge blue one the color of the shell Kawalsky had given me—and brought it home to press in my journal. I thought it would help me come a little closer to Harris, but it didn't work. My brother had gone away from me and the door between us was closed.

Then, during the last week in May, Kurt Shih phoned us with the news that the trial day had been set. He asked us to come on down to his office so we could go over some points.

We met in his office, all of us, including Obaachan, who was so much in awe of the assistant district attorney that she bowed whenever he looked at her.

"I thought you'd like to know the waiting's almost over," he announced in his brittle way. "We're going to trial on July 25—a little less than two months from now."

Dad translated for Obaachan, who once again bowed to Mr. Shih and thanked him in Japanese. "Whoa, Mrs. Mizuno, no need to thank me," Kurt Shih exclaimed. "I haven't started to fight yet, and fight it'll be. This trial will be like a war in more ways than one."

"Because of Silcom and the local hate group?" Dad sounded as brittle as Mr. Shih.

"Among other things. You've got to stay strong and cool, Mr. Mizuno. You've got to promise yourself not to let the Brotherhood of SAW anger you into making some blunder that Ms. Fallister can use to her client's advantage."

"We are behind you one hundred percent." Dad's nostrils were flaring, his eyes blazed dark fire. "I promise there will be no blunders."

"And stay clear of Jerry Cho," Kurt Shih warned. "He can mean trouble for us now that he's up to his old tricks again."

The A.D.A. said that Jerry was well known to the police in L.A. because he'd founded a group called the Asian Power through Unity league. "It was a volatile group—dangerous as hell and totally devoted to Cho," he continued. "A couple of league members almost beat a man to death in L.A. Two of them are serving time, but Cho himself beat the rap and left the West Coast."

The A.D.A. said that Jerry was openly trying to recruit followers and start a new league. "His actions might hurt us in court," Mr. Shih added. "If you have any influence with him, it'd be wise to calm him down," he added.

"I don't believe in vigilante justice either," Dad protested, "but there's nothing I can do. I hardly know the man."

The A.D.A. switched gears and reminded us of another Asian Advancement Group meeting that was coming up in a few days. "It's going to be held in Westriver again," he explained. "Boris has been making plans for his solidarity march in June, and I hope that will help to swing public opinion our way." Dad said nothing. "Have you noticed that the newspaper editorials are almost all in our favor? The last one in the *Westriver Herald* was particularly good."

"Words mean nothing to me. I'm neither a minister nor an activist nor a politician. *I want the man who killed my son.*"

Dad spoke the words in a whisper, but he might as well have roared them out loud. Beside him, Mitch made a gulping sound, and our father reached out and touched his shoulder and then his cheek the way he'd sometimes done to Harris.

"Don't worry, son. We'll see it through together," he promised.

Feeling excluded, feeling alone, I turned away to hide the tears in my eyes. And for once my tears had nothing to do with losing Harris. This time, my sadness was for me.

Since A.D.A. Shih had said we should attend the AAG meeting, Dad packed us all into the car on Thursday and we drove to the Unitarian Church.

We were early. It was a warm evening, which meant that the church would rapidly turn stuffy, and remembering how uncomfortable she'd felt last time we were here, Obaachan said she wanted to walk a little before going inside. So while the folks went into the church to talk with the reverend, Mitch and I stayed outside with Obaachan.

Our grandmother walked slowly, pausing to look at everything. She was especially curious about the Joystick Arcade. "In Japan," she told us, "my grand-chirren play many games in place like this. They take me to play, once."

Obaachan in an arcade? Mitch and I exchanged astonished glances. "Want to try?" Mitch asked.

Our grandmother covered her mouth to hide a laugh and said, oh, no, she was too old for such things. "No, you're not," Mitch exclaimed. "I'll teach you how to play. C'mon, Obaachan, it'll be fun."

As he was trying to persuade her, six or seven men in flak jackets sauntered out of the Joystick. Their heads were shaved, and one of them had a swastika tattooed on his arm.

I nudged Mitch and said, "We'd better go."

Obediently, Obaachan turned, but it was too late. "Hey, lookit, Karo," one of the skinheads yelped. "One old yella bitch and two slanty-eyed pups."

My stomach sank down to the pavement, and I tasted bile. "Start walking," I hissed to Mitch, who'd balled up both fists. "Ignore those creeps."

Mitch didn't budge, so I punched his arm. "You heard what they said about us," he growled.

"So what are you going to do?" I snapped at him. "Quit being stupid."

I hurried Obaachan toward the church, and after a second Mitch, still fuming, joined us. Too late—the skinheads cut us off and stood blocking the way and I now saw that the one called Karo had odd eyes, one brown, the other blue. He was the one who'd stood by the post office handing out leaflets— "Get out of our way," I said, hating the scared quaver I heard in my own voice. "Leave us alone. We've done nothing to you."

Just then a familiar voice spoke. "*There* you are," Mr. Kawalsky said.

I'd never been so glad to see anyone in my life, and my gratitude index edged up a few more notches as I saw Nick had accompanied his dad. We were no longer alone.

Mr. Kawalsky came up to Karo's left ear, which had a skull and crossbones dangling from it. It didn't seem to worry the newspaper editor—in fact he totally ignored Karo. "I've been looking for you everywhere," he said to Mitch and me. "The reverend is waiting for you. Can you use a hand, Mrs. Mizuno?"

Mr. Kawalsky walked up to us, took Obaachan's arm and led her forward, past the skinheads. We followed. Behind us, I could hear a kind of collective intaking of breath as Karo snarled, "I didn't say they could leave."

Mr. Kawalsky turned and looked straight into Karo's mismatched eyes. Almost mildly, he said, "Last I heard, it was a free country. Leave these people alone."

"It's the newshound," one of the skinheads muttered. Karo frowned.

"I'm getting real tired of reading the lies you write in your paper. You want to be careful what garbage you print."

He stuck out a fist, heavy and menacing, and pushed it almost under Mr. Kawalsky's nose. All Mr. Kawalsky said was, "I'm gratified to hear you can read."

Then, turning his back, he and Nick walked us toward the church. I could feel the hairs on my neck prickle as we went, but no one followed us this time.

"Thanks," I managed to whisper when we got to the church steps.

Mr. Kawalsky tapped me lightly on the shoulder.

"For nothing. Okay, Nick—make sure you cover the meeting for me."

"Isn't he going to stay and listen to what goes on?" I asked, as Mr. Kawalsky walked briskly across the street to a parked minivan that said, *Westriver Herald* on the side.

"Nah. There's a selectman's hearing he has to cover in Hanley." Nick shot me a sideways look. "You okay?"

I nodded, but Mitch was fuming. "That—that bastard. Did'ya hear what he said about us? I shoulda nailed him."

"And had your head knocked off," Nick said, before I could. "Those were mean dudes, Mitch. My knees were knocking. Didn't you hear them?"

By now we'd gotten to the church, where Obaachan said she needed to sit down. She hadn't said a word the whole time, but she'd been shaking her head and whispering, *"Arré, arré ma,"* and other unintelligible Japanese words to herself all during our walk to the church.

I guided her to a seat in the back because Rev. Thanh was already talking about the solidarity march.

"It's time for the Asian community to make a stand against the wrongdoing that so often befalls our people. The time for our march is now."

Boom! went the reverend's voice, carrying everyone along as he told us that he'd expanded his ideas for his march.

"We have to be a little cynical," the reverend went on. "We have to be a little calculating. Look, a march in itself is nothing but a group of people waving flags and chanting slogans. Nothing but a band playing and a few speeches. But if the numbers are there, that's another story. It can be magic!"

He reached out his arms as if shouting out a hallelujah. "We're asking our brother and sister Asians and people of good will from all races to come and join us. *Then* we'll have an impressive crowd. And here's some good news: State Senator Buford has expressed interest in addressing us."

State Senator David Buford was youthful, energetic, and the youngest son of a family of politicians. Already, people were comparing him to a young Jack Kennedy. If he was joining the march, Rev. Thanh enthused, we'd really get press coverage and our message would be heard everywhere.

"Will it?" I heard my dad mutter to himself.

"We'll march around Boston Common. There'll be speeches—hopefully a keynote address by Senator Buford. Then a delegation will walk over to Boston's State House and deliver a statement to the governor."

The reverend paused. "I know that hate groups have invaded our town. Harvey Silcom is an evil man who is inflaming local racists and trying to capitalize on the Mizunos' tragedy. But by our numbers, our strength, our togetherness, we'll defeat these servants of the devil."

His voice shook with such conviction that I could almost feel it sear me. Before us, the church hummed with approval and agreement. It seemed so simple when Rev. Thanh said it, but then, Rev. Thanh hadn't been face to face with Karo. He hadn't seen the hate in Karo's wild eyes.

Later, when we all gathered together after the meeting, Mom was enthusiastic about the march. Dad didn't say much about it and instead thanked Nick for rescuing us from the skinheads.

"My mother told me how it happened," he said. "I'm grateful to you and your father, but I wish I'd been there to face these men who insulted my family."

He offered Nick a ride home, but my friend asked to be dropped off at the newspaper office, a few blocks away. "I want to write up my notes on tonight's meeting," he explained.

"Ah, you are a good son. You help your father in his work."

Approval mixed with longing in Dad's voice, but

Mom's mind was on another trail. "I hate to think of what might have happened if Mr. Kawalsky hadn't happened to come by when he did," she said. "I can't thank you enough, Nick."

Nick blushed and said it was no big deal. "We'd just parked the van when we saw the skinheads walking out of the Joystick," he explained. Then, as Dad started to drive toward the newspaper office, Nick added, "What I can't believe is that nobody else even tried to help you—"

Nick's words broke off as there was this massive, earth-shattering boom. "What was *that*?" Mom gasped.

"It sounded like an explosion." Dad put pedal to metal and screeched our car around a corner. As we turned it, we saw smoke and some flames billowing out of a building further down on South Street.

"Oh, my God," Nick shouted. "It's the *Herald!*"

Nick grabbed for the door handle and tumbled out of our still moving car. I yelled at him, but paying me no mind he started running. My dad screeched the car to a halt, jumped out, and took off after Nick. He caught him in a running tackle and held him down.

"*No*, Nick," Dad shouted.

Leaving Obaachan in the safety of the car, Mitch, Mom, and I ran over to them. "My dad," Nick was sobbing, and as if to emphasize his desolation, a dog began to howl nearby. "Let go of me," Nick pleaded. "My dad may be still *in* there."

Now sirens were screeching down the street toward us. Nick pushed himself free of Dad's grasp and started running down the street again. As we all hastened in pursuit, I saw something dark staggering out of the burning building.

"Dad!" Nick shrieked.

The shadowy figure buckled at the knees and pitched forward onto the pavement. We all ran after Nick who reached his father first and fell to his knees beside the still body.

"Nick," Mr. Kawalsky moaned.

Mr. Kawalsky's eyes were open. His eyebrows and eyelashes had been singed off, and his cheeks were black with soot. "The *Herald*—have to save the *Herald*."

He tried to get up, but Dad held him down. "Did the skinheads do this?" he cried.

"I don't know—"

Mr. Kawalsky's voice trailed away. Behind us, the office of the *Westriver Herald* burned. Somewhere in the darkness that dog howled again.

"What's happening with that dog? It sounds hurt," I heard Mitch mutter distractedly, but I didn't have time to answer because right then the paramedics and the firefighters arrived. So did the police, who began cordoning off the area.

Pushed to one side, we watched as they hustled Mr. Kawalsky into the ambulance. A woman police officer, introducing herself as Sergeant Gady, drew Dad and Mom aside and asked them if they'd seen or heard anyone just after the explosion.

I went over to Kawalsky, who was waiting by the ambulance. "I'm going with my dad," he said, and there was a look on his face that was beyond scared, a look I totally understood. He'd lost his mom, not many years ago—no use telling him it would be all right. Both of us knew that death made a mockery of those words.

"What can I do?" I asked, aching for him, but Nick didn't even hear me. He started following the paramedics and then stopped to turn his tortured, frightened face toward me. He couldn't speak, and neither could I except to plead, "Hang on, Nick. Please, hang on, okay?"

Then the ambulance was screaming away. I turned to find Mitch and saw that he was gone, too. "Oh, for Pete's sake," I moaned. "The idiot's gone to look for the dog."

Dad and Mom were still talking to Sergeant Gady.

I ducked past them and looked up and down the street, which was crawling with cops and rubberneckers leaning over to get a good look. There were people all over but no sign of my dumb younger brother.

Calling his name, I walked down the street toward the park. There was no answer, and the park was silent. I hesitated, wondering if I should look for Mitch in there. It looked pretty dark and deserted, but if I were a hurt dog, I'd hide amongst dark and deserted trees, wouldn't I? And Mitch, who often thought like the animals he loved, would look in the park first.

As I started down the walkway that led into the park, I thought of what Dad would do to me if he knew I was traipsing around the park on my own. I'd just about decided to turn back and get some help when I heard someone cough up ahead.

Mitch? I started to yell his name, stopped in case it wasn't Mitch at all. Cautiously, I rounded a bend in the path and found myself near the park pond. It glistened ominously in the park lights and the trees that surrounded it threw giant shadows.

"Mitch?" I whispered.

Then I nearly fainted as somebody got up from a park bench near the lake. It was a man—I could see the outline of heavy shoulders, of a beefy body bending slightly forward as if ready to chase me if I ran. I *wanted* to run, but my legs wouldn't move.

The man took a step toward me. "Stay away," I wanted to shout, but my words came out in a low moan.

"Who's there? What do you want?"

His voice was as scared as mine—and familiar. I'd never heard him talk in person, but I'd heard him on TV lots of times. My already churning stomach did a sickening flip as I realized that the man confronting me here in the darkness was Rodney Waring.

EIGHT

WARING'S HANDS WERE hanging at his sides, his head was pushed forward, peering through the darkness at me. We were alone.

I wanted to spit in his face. To tell him what kind of slimy lowlife he was. I'd fantasized this moment so often for so long, and now all the things I'd ever dreamed of doing to the man who'd murdered Harris crowded into my mind and I couldn't think of what to say or do first.

"Who's there?" Waring demanded again. "I can't see too good." Then, in a voice that jumped with nerves, he rasped, "What you standing there so quiet, for? Cat got your tongue?"

"I'm Terri Mizuno," I snarled. "You shot my brother."

He didn't say anything, but he sort of quivered—as if somebody'd zapped him with an electric charge. "What do you want?" he then said, his voice real loud, blustering. "You keep away from me, or I'll have the cops on you."

It hit me suddenly that he was scared of *me*. A sense of bitter power raged through me, carrying me forward like a cork on a dark wave. I took a step forward. Two—

He retreated quavering, "Go away—get out of here. I've got a right to walk in the park if I want to."

"Harris can't walk in the park," I reminded him. "He won't ever have a cup of coffee or play soccer or go to Harvard. You took care of that."

"Leave me alone." Waring rasped. "Leave me the hell alone!"

Leave *him* alone after what he'd done to my family? But before I could blast him, he'd turned and started shambling away. Strange, he'd looked big and tough and healthy on the TV program, but his walk was that of an old man.

No way was I going to let him get away. I ran after him, catching up to him as he stepped onto the path that skirted the pond in the park. "I want you to know," I told him, "what you took away from us that night. I want you to think about this, you—you creep. If it wasn't for you, Harris would be alive right now."

"Don't you think I know it?"

Waring didn't turn around, but I saw his rounded shoulders heave—with anger or pain or despair—who knew? "I think about it every minute of the day," he went on. "Every single minute, I go over what I done that night. Every minute."

"You murdered my brother," I accused.

"Didn't mean to." Slowly, he turned, and I saw the heavy outline of his face gleam pale in the new moonlight. "So help me, Jesus, I didn't mean to."

"So now you're going to tell me you blow away everybody who comes to your door," I rapped out at him. My hands were clenched, and I was shaking with the hate that raged in me like hurricane wind. "Who do you think you are, Clint Eastwood, huh? Wyatt Earp? My brother just wanted to use the phone, that's why he came to your door, and you murdered him!"

I'd wanted to scream the last words at him, but hate had solidified into a lump in my throat, and my voice couldn't push past it. It didn't matter, anyway, because Waring wasn't listening to me.

In a low, hollow, rusty voice he was saying, "Like I told the cops. Like I told them. He come running down the driveway, wrapped up in that black raincoat. He had the hood over his head and he looked big. Mean. He pounded on the door and wouldn't go

110

away. I'll call the police,' Janey says, but the cops don't come quick enough to make no never mind."

The words stumbled out of him in a monotonous murmur, one sentence following the other, on and on, as if he wasn't talking to me, but to himself. As if what he'd seen and done that night was doing a slow-motion replay in front of his eyes. I listened, almost hypnotized by the horrible rhythm of his words until he said, "Then I went and got my gun."

"And with that damned gun you shot my brother!" Once more I tried to shout, but the words came out in a strangled whisper.

"He knocks and knocks. Knocks and knocks. Wham, wham, wham—" The man's hands pantomimed slamming on wood. "Janey begun to cry. I said, don't worry, this time the bastard won't hurt you, honey. And then he knocks so hard I'm afraid he's going to come through the door, and Janey screams, and I shoot him."

Silence, now, and far away the police and fire sirens. "Why?" I tried to ask, but the word wouldn't pass the blockage in my throat.

"I thought he was going to hurt Janey. So help me, Jesus, I did think that. Hurt her like she'd been hurt before. Week ago, a big guy, six foot plus, he jumped her at the mall down to Hanley, pushed her down, grabbed her purse. Kicked her in the ribs—broke three." He drew shuddering breath. "Broke three ribs, the bastard, and now she can't take a breath without pain."

One thing had nothing to do with the other. I tried to cloak myself in my hate for Waring, but suddenly, it didn't seem quite so impenetrable, and the lump in my throat tasted like sewage. Without the armor of my anger I felt naked and cold.

Hastily, I pulled it close around me again. "I don't want to listen to you." I whipped around to walk away, but his toneless voice pursued me.

"I see what happened that night all the time. Every

111

day, every minute. Over and over, like a movie in hell. When I dream at night, I try and make it so I don't shoot that boy, try to pull my hand back in time, but it don't do no good."

He put his hand up to his eyes, dragged his sleeve across them. "It don't do no good," he repeated wearily. "When I wake up, he's still dead."

"But you're alive," I said, trying to goad the hate back, "and that *boy* is dead."

"I'd change places in a second," he came right back. "So help me Jesus, I would."

I covered my ears with my hands. "I don't believe you," I yelled. "Don't think Ms. Fallister will get you off so's you can share in her book and TV rights. I hope they put you in jail for the rest of your life."

Just then, there was a noise of footsteps in the near distance. "Terri—Ter-ree Mizuno!" a familiar voice called.

With the yellow eye of a flashlight winking before him, Damon Ying came down the path. Grateful that he was there, that he'd cared enough to come looking for me, I called, "Here—I'm here, Damon."

Damon shone the flashlight on us and started walking toward the pond. "Your folks are going nuts looking for you," he started to say. Then he saw that someone was with me, shone the flashlight in Waring's face. "Well," he exclaimed, "I'll be damned. Look who joined the party, Jerry."

There was a footstep behind him, and I saw Jerry Cho come out of the darkness to stand beside Damon. He didn't say a word, but his nostrils flared as if he'd smelled something he didn't like.

"You leave me alone," Waring blustered. "I done nothing to you. You just leave me alone."

"The great Rodney Waring in person," Damon said. He flipped the flashlight up and down, so that the light danced over Waring. "What were you doing out here alone, old man? Rehearsing your next speech to the press? Figuring what you're going to say next

me you're on TV? Or maybe what you're going to say
Harvey Silcom next time the big man comes here to
ake your hand?"

"Not gonna do no more TV," Waring mumbled. Im-
led by the bright eye of the flashlight, he looked
ffy and pale. "I told that lawyer, I ain't doing no
ore of that stuff."

"You don't need to now that you're buddy-buddy
ith the SAW," Jerry Cho said. He walked forward
owly, keeping his eyes on Waring all the while. "But
w we have you alone, don't we? No lawyer, no hate
oups, no reporters. Just you and us."

Rodney Waring got even paler, and his eyes darted
ke scared fish. "You don't dare do nothing to me," he
avered.

Jerry Cho's voice rose sharply. "The *system* isn't go-
g to do anything to you. But I'm not the system, am
Am I, old man?"

As I watched Jerry move closer to Waring, my heart
egan to hammer. My mouth had gone dry. "Was it
n killing that Jap boy?" Cho asked softly. "Did it feel
od?"

"I ain't going to talk to you." Terror distorted War-
g's voice into a bleat. "I'm leaving, now. You can't
op me."

Moving so swiftly that it was like a blur, Jerry Cho
t in front of Waring, cutting off his way of escape.
e tried to go the other way but Damon blocked him.
Now what're you going to do, old man?"

Waring did a dance of terror, trying to get around
erry Cho and then whirling to try to escape Damon.
ouldn't. He was panting with fear, and in the flash-
ght that Damon kept spotlighted on Waring's face, I
w that he was sweating like mad.

It was ugly. Scary. "Jerry, maybe you'd better stop,"
heard my own uncertain voice say.

"I'll stop when Waring confesses that he murdered
ur brother in cold blood," Jerry said. "I'm not mov-
g till he tells the truth."

113

Waring gave a strangled noise. This was the minut
I'd prayed for, the moment of my revenge. I shoul
have been glad to witness Waring's fear, but I fel
sickened instead. In a louder voice I said, "Wha
you're doing—this isn't right."

"Right?" Damon swiveled on his heel toward me
"Right?" he repeated in a disbelieving voice. "This i
the guy who killed your brother, and you're taking hi
side?"

I protested, "I'm not on his side, I'm not! But I don'
think it's right to—to do this to him. He says he—he
says he didn't mean to kill Harris."

I actually heard myself say those words. *He says he
didn't mean to kill Harris.* Words that had shattere
friendship between Melanie Reed and me—impossible
that I was even admitting the possibility myself.

"Are you messed in the head? Of course he'd *say*
that," Damon snapped. Jerry Cho gave an ugly little
laugh.

"Women are weak. Cry a little, and they'll believe
anything you say. But I'm no woman, Waring. I want
you to walk with me down to the police station and
tell them you killed the Mizuno boy in cold blood.
That'll send your friends from the SAW slithering
back under their rocks. It'll end this circus. So let's do
it. Now!"

Jerry's voice rose in a shout. Waring made a sound
like a dry hasp squalking open. In the cold light of
Damon's flashlight, Waring's mouth was slack and
open, like a fish. Ineffectually, his hands opened and
closed at his sides.

It was sickening to watch. I turned my head, re-
minding myself that Waring *was* guilty and not just of
Harris's death, either. I had a vivid mental flash of
Karo threatening us, of flames and fire and Mr.
Kawalsky lying on the pavement, of Obaachan and
me crouching behind the bed.

"Your folks are worried for you, Terri. You'd better

114

go join them." Jerry Cho was talking to me, but he didn't take his eyes off Waring.

I knew I should turn my back and walk away. Left alone, Jerry would get a confession out of Waring. A guilty plea would end this craziness, make sure that Waring went to prison. Who cared what methods Jerry used? It was what the creep deserved.

"An eye for an eye makes the world blind—" As I whispered those words, I heard voices coming toward us and Dad's voice calling my name.

"Be quiet and let them pass," Jerry warned, but I was already shouting.

"Here—here I am!"

Jerry cursed loudly, then stepped aside so that Waring could blunder past him and shamble away into the darkness. "Damn it," Jerry raged. "*Damn* it. One minute longer, and he'd have confessed. We'd have *had* him." He turned angrily to me. "Why'd you call them over here for? What's the matter with you?"

Damon was shaking his head. "I can't *believe* it," he gritted. "I can't believe you, Terri, letting that murderer wriggle off the hook." He gave me a cold, dark look. "I was wrong about you. You're not strong, you don't have pride. You're a coward. You're nothing."

By now flashlights were bobbing toward us. First came my dad, and then Mitch, and a bunch of police officers led by Sergeant Gady.

"Terri, you okay?" Mitch shrilled, running up to me. I nodded, wordless, as Damon started telling my dad that he and Jerry had just now stumbled across me.

"She was just standing here by the pond. She must still be in shock because of what happened at the *Herald* office," he added glibly. "Right, Terri?"

There was an unspoken warning in his voice not to tell of the scene with Waring. Dad was asking. "Why were you out here? Why did you worry all of us by disappearing? Answer me!"

His voice kept rising, and he looked furious. "I—was looking for Mitch," I mumbled.

"Looking for him all by yourself in the park?" Dad exploded. "With those skinheads all over? *Bakayaro!*" he shouted at me.

I felt the sting of that word even more than I'd have felt a slap. To be called "horse deer" might mean nothing to your average American, but I knew that it was the worst insult in Dad's book. I felt worthless, loathsome, no better than slime.

In a scared voice, Mitch said, "I'm sorry I took off, Terri. I found this dog—it'd got lost in all the confusion, I guess. I had to find its owners and make sure it was okay." He paused not meeting my eyes and mumbled, "Sorry I got you into trouble."

Ignoring both of us, Dad walked over and shook Damon's and Jerry's hands. "It's lucky you found her and not—not someone else."

As Damon protested that it was nothing, Sergeant Gady asked, suddenly, "What *were* you two doing in the park at this time of night?"

"We were at the Joystick Arcade when we heard something explode," Cho said blandly. "Damon and I ran over to see what'd happened. Then we heard Terri Mizuno was missing and so we joined the search."

"Then you weren't trying to round up some suspects on your own?" Sergeant Gady persisted.

"*Have* you found the men responsible?" Dad interrupted so curtly that Sergeant Gady frowned. Sounding brusque herself, she replied that she was looking into it.

Dad muttered something I couldn't catch under his breath, rapped a command at Mitch and me, and stalked away.

Wordless as dogs called to heel, we followed and joined Mom, who first hugged me and then yelled at me, and Obaachan, who clicked her teeth and shook her head as if I were a hopeless case. Then I sat through the car ride home during which my dad lectured me on how incredibly thoughtless, irresponsible, and immature I'd been.

116

"The police had to divert some of their men to finding you," he seethed. "Perhaps those extra men would have been able to catch the criminals."

I'd seen Dad mad before, but never like this. I mumbled I was sorry, but he didn't even hear me. I wondered what he'd have done if he heard that I'd helped Waring stay in one piece tonight. Probably order me to commit hara-kiri.

"I'm really sorry, Terri," Mitch whispered from beside me in the car. "He ripped *me* up and down pretty good, too."

But had Dad taken Mitch apart as he'd done me? Would he have yelled at Harris, or Alice as he'd yelled at me? I didn't think so. As usual, I'd infuriated him. As usual, I had disappointed and disgraced him. I'd never measure up in my father's eyes, never amount to anything—and maybe he was right.

I wanted to cry in hurt and humiliation, but guilt kept my eyes dry. And when we got home, I went straight up the stairs to my room. Correction: my *shared* room. In my misery, I'd forgotten about Obaachan. I'd just plopped down on my bed to have a good cry when the little old lady walked in.

"Take bedcover *off* before you lie down," she directed.

I was in no mood for her lectures. What I wanted was someplace to hide. I needed to dig myself a hole where no one would see me, where I didn't have to think about anything that had happened tonight.

About Damon, and how he had turned on me. About Rodney Waring crying while he talked about Harris. About Dad yelling at me and humiliating me in front of everyone when what I'd needed most was a hug.

I slid off the bed and was heading for the door when Obaachan called me back. "I know you worried, Terri-chan," she said. "Just now your mama call hospital. Mr. Kawalsky is in the good condition. Being treated for smoke in-har-ation."

Selfishly, I'd forgotten all about Mr. Kawalsky. I

thought of Nick, waiting for word of his father. "It stinks," I muttered.

"Mr. Kawalsky is brave, strong man. Office building can be repaired." Unexpectedly, she reached out to pat my hand. "Don't too much worry."

Angry footsteps punished the stairs, and I tensed as Dad strode past our room. He didn't stop, though, and soon there was the noise of a door slamming. Obaachan sighed. "Juntaro too much worried. He thinking you hurt bad. So, when he finds you, he is angry. He is yelling. It is what all man does."

"Not all," I muttered.

"All mans," Obaachan reiterated firmly. "Juntaro's father was same. When he gets worried, he don't want to admit weakness. So he scold and shout." Obaachan paused for a long moment, and I figured she was through. But then she said somberly, "It is not good."

"No, it's not," I mumbled, but as if she hadn't heard, Obaachan went on speaking.

"Juntaro was always good boy," she sighed. "Kind in heart. Now, he is angry, very hard. He becoming like—"

She didn't finish the sentence. Didn't have to. From the way her eyes sought out one of the photos on her spirit altar, I knew that she'd been going to say, "Juntaro is becoming like his father."

With another deep sigh, Obaachan knelt down on the floor. Slowly, very slowly, she picked up her little bell. "Not good to be so angry inside," she murmured. "Juntaro is changing from boy I used to know. I am afraid for him."

Next morning the reporters were back. We watched them hanging out on our front yard, chatting and drinking coffee from Styrofoam cups, and Mitch growled, "I'd like to pop them one. Mr. Kawalsky's hurt, and all they can think about is headlines."

At least Mr. Kawalsky was going to be all right. Mom had called the hospital and found out that he

118

was off the critical list. "But those arsonists meant business."

I looked down at the newspaper on the breakfast table. "NEWSPAPER OFFICE FIREBOMBED, EDITOR HURT," the headlines blared. "MIZUNO SHOOTING BREEDS MORE VIOLENCE."

Not the racist Brotherhood of the SAW, mind you, not Mr. Harvey Silcom cranking out sick hatred from his plush office in New Orleans, but the Mizunos. The newspapers sounded as if *we* were responsible for spreading violence.

"It's getting dangerous." Dad looked hard at me as he added, "I want to know where you children are twenty-four hours a day. No more surprises. After school you get on the school bus and come home. Straight into the house."

"Jun," Mom said worriedly, "I think we need police protection. If we talk to Kurt Shih—"

"I can take care of my own family, Laura."

He was using the high-and-mighty tone that always got Mom's goat. But instead of flaring up, she just stared at her breakfast plate. "We couldn't protect Harris," she whispered.

Abruptly Dad got up and walked out of the room. Mom gave her head a little shake as if pushing away shadows and cobwebs. "It was lucky Damon Ying found you last night in the park, Terri."

Warily, I nodded. "I know Damon was a friend of Harris's," Mom went on, "but I don't think it's wise for you kids to hang around with Jerry Cho. You know what Mr. Shih said about him."

"Aw, Ma," Mitch scoffed, "Jerry's okay. And he's better than Bruce Lee, even. Remember how he jumped those skinheads at the funeral?"

His eyes glowed with hero worship, but Mom wasn't paying attention. Instead, she was looking at me. "Damon's a very charismatic young man," she said, "but he *is* older. I don't know if you should spend too much

119

time with him, Terri. He'll be off to college in the fall, while you'll just be a junior."

Poor Mom, with her mind on romance. Her mother's intuition had zeroed in on my crush on Damon, but her antennae were operating on time delay. After last night, I knew Damon would never look at me again.

Had I been wrong to call out when I did and stop Jerry from tormenting Waring? I didn't know. Thinking of what had happened made me feel sick inside, so I looked out at the milling reporters outside. Mitch was eyeing them darkly. "Yeah, well," he went, "I wish Damon was here to face those newshounds, boy. He could run right through them, and—lookit—there's Mrs. Despard talking to one of them. Maybe she's going to call the cops on *him*."

We had our work cut out for us beating a path through the press, and we just barely caught the bus to school. When we got there, I didn't see Kawalsky, so I worried about him. I wanted to go to Xavier Hospital after school, but I was so sure Dad would veto the idea that I didn't even ask him if we could go. But, surprise, surprise, my father came home early from work to go to the hospital himself.

"It is the least I can do," he said, and I knew he was thinking of Mr. Kawalsky facing down Karo and his friends and wondering if that confrontation had led to the *Herald*'s being set on fire.

I asked if I could go, too, and, after a second, Dad nodded. I hoped that this was a sign that he regretted tearing into me last night, but then he said, "If I don't take you, you'll probably go by yourself and get into trouble."

We didn't say a word to each other en route to the hospital, and the tension between us rasped like steel wool by the time we'd reached Mr. Kawalsky's room. There Nick was sitting by his dad's bed, playing checkers with him.

Like a fool, I asked Mr. Kawalsky how he felt. I

mean, there he was with his head bandaged, a plaster over the bridge of his nose, his right hand in a cast, and two black eyes. He could still smile though. "I feel," he said, "as if I tangled with a concrete mixer." Then he added, "I'm also glad to be alive."

Nick offered Dad his chair. "I feel guilty," my father said, sitting down and shaking Mr. Kawalsky's good hand. "You were targeted because of your sympathies to my family."

While Dad was talking, Nick motioned me outside. He looked tired and so pale that the freckles on his nose stood out darkly. "You okay?" I asked.

"It was pretty rough last night," he admitted. "They let me sleep in a cot near Dad's bed, but I didn't close my eyes because I was scared that he—" He broke off. "You know."

I nodded. I knew.

He exhaled a long breath. "Yeah," he said, "well, he's going to be okay, and we found out that the *Herald* office wasn't that badly damaged, either. Some repairs and it'll be as good as new."

He paused. "Your dad doesn't have to feel guilty, Terri. My old man just writes what he believes in, that's all. He'd have written those editorials come hell or high water."

His voice was warm with exasperated pride and affection, and I remembered how I'd felt when Dad yelled at me last night in the park. "My father has a thing about honor and stuff like that," I said, trying to make a joke of it, "but to him it means something different. It's what we kids call 'the Japanese Thing.'"

"Everything means something different to different people," Nick mumbled, then stopped to crack a huge yawn. "Did I really say that? I must be getting punchy."

We proceeded to walk down the corridor together, and though he didn't say much, I felt my friend's frustration and his anger. "They'll get the creeps who did it," I assured him.

"We all *know* who did it. They're probably running

121

around boasting about what they did." Kawalsky's usually mild face was hard as he burst out, "I hate the Brotherhood of the SAW. I hate the lousy Society of Aryan Warriors. I hope that slick sleaze Silcom fries in hell for what he did to Dad."

"That's how I—" I began, and stopped.

I'd been about to say that this was how I'd *felt* about Rodney Waring. Past tense. "That's how I *feel* about Waring," I said defiantly.

Nick looked at me sideways. I knew what that look meant. Anyone else would have taken my words at face value. Anyone else in Nick's position would have been so wrapped up in his own problems that he wouldn't have had time to bother about anyone else.

"I don't want to talk about it," I said, to that questioning look.

He just nodded. He wasn't going to pry, I thought, relieved, as I tried to steer him back to talking about Mr. Kawalsky, and Nick said that the *Herald* was most probably bombed because of the last editorial Mr. Kawalsky had written.

"Groups like SAW hate the thought of the truth," he added. "They can't deal with it, so they'd rather kill and destroy."

"Like Jerry and Damon."

I wasn't sure whether I'd thought it or said it aloud, but Nick looked surprised. "Really? I mean Damon's got this macho thing about being a hero, but I don't think he'd kill or destroy anybody."

"Last night—" I broke off, gulped, and then said it. "While I was looking for Mitch, I met Waring in the park."

Nick was so shocked that he could hardly talk. "You met *Waring*?" He grabbed me by the arms, hauled me off to a bench near a window, and pulled me down to sit beside him. "Oh, man, oh, man! What happened?"

So I told him. I guess I had to tell someone—the memory of that whole scene was just too much to handle alone. "The thing was," I finished, "I actually almost believed him. Can you believe I could be that crazy?"

Nick had been sitting there just staring at me. "Oh, man, that is *scary*," he finally said. "That's exactly how I felt toward *him*. You know, the guy who slammed into my mom and killed her."

It was my turn to stare. Nick knuckled his hands into fists and pounded them onto his knees as he went on, "Yeah. Right. *Him*—the drunk. The bum. The guy I was going to kill with my bare hands. Only, when I saw him in court, he looked small and sick, and he was crying."

Nick looked ready to cry himself. I bowed my head so as to hide my own tears. "I thought there was something wrong in me—I mean, not to hate Waring the way I used to."

"Then there's something wrong with me, too. No matter how I tried to think of what he'd done to Mom—to us—I couldn't go on hating that guy." Nick quit pounding his knees to add, "I felt like—you know—I was selling out. It made me so nuts, I told Dad, and he said he was glad." *Glad?* "He said I had to let it go and move on."

He paused. "Maybe you need to tell your folks about meeting Waring, Terri."

I thought of my father's anger last night and said nothing. Nick didn't push it. "So what else happened?" he wanted to know.

About to relate what had happened next, I hesitated. Somehow, I couldn't bear to talk about what had happened when Damon and Jerry Cho joined us.

So I suggested we go back to Mr. Kawalsky's room. When we got there, my dad was standing by the bed talking to Rev. Thanh and another man. The newcomer's back was to the door, so all I could see was that he had dark blond hair and wore a handsome gray suit.

Rev. Thanh hailed Nick and me in his river-deep voice. "I stopped by to see Mr. Kawalsky," he told us.

"That such a thing should happen to us in Westriver—it's outrageous! It makes our solidarity march even more important, and I'm glad to say that Senator Buford agrees."

Rev. Thanh was so pleased that he almost sang the name. Now the man in the gray suit had turned to look at us, and I recognized the by-now famous smile and earnest blue eyes.

"Your daughter, Mr. Mizuno?" Senator Buford asked Dad. "A clever young lady. I read your piece in the *Boston Globe*," he added as he shook my hand. "It was what made me contact Reverend Thanh."

The reverend beamed. Dad said, "Oh, my daughter is not clever at all," in a way that made me sure that for once he wasn't being modest out of politeness.

Senator Buford had a strong handshake. He gave me his full attention for nearly a minute and then turned to Nick, congratulating him for his presence of mind last night. "You have a courageous father," he said. "He tells us that the *Westriver Herald* is going to be back in business by the end of the week."

"The press must roll on," the reverend said approvingly. "We need you to cover the solidarity march in two weeks' time, Reg. We've already had calls from Vermont and New Hampshire, and now that Senator Buford has agreed to be the keynote speaker, our numbers will increase by leaps and bounds."

For a second he looked as if he were going to break into the "Hallelujah Chorus," but instead he turned practical. "We'll be needing volunteers to help paint signs, make and field telephone calls. I hope we can count on you young people?"

Nick glanced at his father and then agreed. Dad asked abruptly, "Reverend Thanh, Senator, with all due respect, what *good* will this march do?"

He started to walk around the room, his words emerging not in his usual, carefully thought out sentences but as jerky, half-formed phrases. "I've said all along that I have doubts—we're dealing with criminals here. Barbarians. People who don't have a conscience. All they respect is force—"

"The march will show hate groups that there's no room for them in this state," the senator intervened. "We mean to show solidarity with our Asian brothers and sisters in the fight against violence and hatred."

He *looked* sincere, but the words had the pat ring of a politician's speech. I remembered what Damon had said about A.D.A. Shih, then resolutely pushed away the memory. The less I thought of Damon the better.

"What's to prevent the SAW racists from having a countermarch on the same day?" Dad demanded.

"Actually, they did apply for a permit to march in the Boston Common on the same day as us, and they were refused," Rev. Thanh said. "I'm more worried about Jerry Cho."

According to the reverend, Jerry Cho was doing a lot of talking amongst restless youths in the Asian community. "He uses his anger to draw other angry people to him. It's my understanding that he's begun to recruit a following."

Suddenly, he thumped himself solidly on his chest. "Anger begins inside *us*, Mr. Mizuno. If we can control ourselves and our tendencies toward violence, eventually there will be no more violence. If there is beauty in the person, there will be harmony in the house. And if there is harmony in the house, there will be order in the nation. And if there is order in the nation, there will be peace in the world."

"A fine-sounding philosophy," Dad said. His eyes added, *but I don't buy it*.

"You'll march with us, Mr. Mizuno?" the senator interposed in his most persuasive voice. "You and your family are our reasons for marching. We *need* you."

Dad hesitated for a moment before nodding wordlessly. He then shook hands with everyone and stalked out of the hospital room.

I said my own good-byes and ran after Dad, who was already punching the down button on the hospital elevator. "Fools," he growled, as I joined them. "Idealistic fools. Jerry Cho has the right idea even if he *is* breaking the law. Evil people only fear force. They respect nothing else."

In a way, I envied my dad. His hate was still hot and strong. He didn't stop to ask himself questions to which there were no answers.

When we got home, I stopped in the kitchen to greet Obaachan, learned that Mitch and Mom were out shopping together, and then climbed the stairs to my blessedly (if temporarily) empty room. If ever there was a time I needed to be alone to write in my journal, this was it.

I pulled out the by now well-fingered notebook, sat down at my desk, and stared at the last entry, which read: "I will hate Rodney Waring till I die."

I closed my journal and rested my arms on my desk and put my head on my arms. I felt so confused. Thousands of thoughts darted like piranha fish in my brain, but at the same time I felt emptied out, as if not hating Waring as wholeheartedly as I'd done before had left an awful void in me. The void had to be filled. The question was, filled with what?

More hate? Easy to do considering the skinheaded brotherhood with their bigotry and their sick ideas. I could easily fill my brain with hatred for people like Link Lewis, but instead, I thought of Rev. Thanh and his peace march.

Peace starting in my own mind—it sounded too good to be true. "Dad's right," I muttered to the silent room. "It'll never work."

" ' 'Tis better to have loved and lost / Than never to have loved at all.' Bet you didn't know that was by Tennyson, huh?"

The familiar voice slid into my mind, rested there like the ghost of a sigh. *Harris?* For a second I was so stunned that I couldn't even open my eyes, and then reality returned. Harris, I thought, sadly, you're not

126

real. You're just my own wishful thinking. You're dead.

And why am I dead? the imaginary voice persisted. *Because I was shot by a man filled with enough fear and hate to make him forget he was human.*

Muted as shadows, soft as smoke, the voice—the thought?—grazed my mind. Would Rodney Waring have pulled that trigger if he hadn't hated the purse snatcher who'd hurt his wife? *Good girl, Terr. Now you're on the right track.* No, he wouldn't have. He wouldn't have had the hate in him, the hate that made him get his gun and shoot me. *And what about you? Don't you have some of that awful hate inside you, too?*

Not me, no way. If I was full of that kind of hate, would I have tried to stop Damon and Jerry from tormenting Waring? If I'd had that hate in me, wouldn't I have enjoyed watching Waring being pushed around?

Why wouldn't you have enjoyed it? That's what you've been wanting, Terr. See? It's in you, too, that hate.

No!

I jerked myself bolt upright at my desk. "No," I repeated aloud, "Damon and Jerry wouldn't have hurt Waring. Jerry was just trying to scare the old guy."

But I didn't know that. I didn't know that at all.

Because I did have the darkness in me, too, and I could see how it might have happened. Had to admit that once I would really have enjoyed watching Waring in pain.

Once more I looked at the journal on my desk. "All right, Harris," I sighed, "you win."

Then I opened up my notebook and began to write.

NINE

Perched on the edge of an uncomfortable metal folding chair in the Kawalskys' basement, I watched tensely as Nick's father scanned the single typewritten page I'd just handed him.

I'd never been so nervous in my life. When Mr. Kawalsky frowned, my heart bucked. Who did I think I was, believing that anyone could be interested in the junk I'd written?

"It's probably dumb," I muttered.

"Nope—not at all." Mr. Kawalsky glanced up momentarily to smile. "Quite the reverse, actually."

Nick nodded encouragingly to me from across the room where he and Mitch were setting up file cabinets. Mitch was absorbed in what he was doing, but Nick had kept his eye on his dad and me.

Until the *Herald* office could be repaired, Mr. Kawalsky had set up temporary headquarters in his own basement. Mitch and I were helping him and Nick get settled. I'd also, at Nick's urging, handed Mr. Kawalsky the distillation of what I'd written after that confrontation with Waring in the park.

"Are you going to print it in the *Herald*, Dad?" Nick wanted to know.

"I have a better idea." Mr. Kawalsky rubbed the edge of his nose with his good hand. "Terri, why don't you read this essay at the solidarity march next week?"

"*Read* it?" I squeaked. "You mean, read it aloud in front of the senator and all those people?"

128

Just then there was a strange, scraping sound outside. We all tensed until Mr. Kawalsky said, "It's just somebody passing by."

Nick, his mouth a tight line, walked up the stairs, listened at the basement door, and then went up into the house. "Should we go with him?" Mitch asked me uncertainly, but just then Nick came downstairs again.

"Nobody was there," he said.

We all breathed more easily. "We're all getting a little paranoid," Mr. Kawalsky sighed. "We see enemies behind trees and under the kitchen sink. Maybe we should rent Walker from you, Mitch."

Walker was feeling his oats pretty much these days. Since Dad had announced that Walker was a good watchdog and an asset to the family, Mitch had spent a week building an elaborate doghouse. He had lugged out one of Mom's best blankets to warm the doghouse floor, and then started on a career scarfing the best parts of our dinner to fill Walker's bowl.

"I wish Walker could give us a hand setting up," Nick said. He looked around the basement, which was cluttered with file cabinets, a desk, Mr. Kawalsky's word processor, and a lot of electronic equipment. "This is one humongous mess."

As the guys got back to work, Mr. Kawalsky picked up the paper again. " 'A single golden rose is growing in the garden,' " he quoted, " 'and it is elegant in its perfection, spotless until a speck of soot chances to fall on it. But it's such a tiny speck, a pinhead of darkness, so nobody pays any attention. But then more and more soot falls, as inexorable as the approach of night—' "

He broke off. "I like the analogy, Terri, but maybe you want to rewrite that last sentence. It's a little overdone."

Embarrassed but grateful, I listened to Mr. Kawalsky's constructive criticism.

"I also like this passage: 'A hundred specks of soot

129

will blot out the beauty of the rose. How much hate will it take to extinguish the light of reason inside a person?'" Mr. Kawalsky paused. "What made you write this, Terri?"

I mumbled that it was some stuff from my journal. "You write well," Mr. Kawalsky then said. "You have a reporter's keen eye and a gift for culling images. I like the way you put words together."

He tapped my essay on his knee. "Have you ever thought of making a career out of writing, Terri?"

Astonished, I shook my head. "She's going to be a lawyer," Mitch piped up. "She's always wanted to be one."

About to agree with Mitch, I suddenly stopped and thought about it. Had I really wanted to go into law all my life or had it been assumed that this was what I was going to do? "It's pretty much what everybody expects me to be," I said aloud.

Mr. Kawalsky was looking at my essay again. "Has your father seen this, Terri?" he asked. When I shook my head, he said, "I think you should show it to him before we show it to Boris Thanh."

"Why's that?" Nick asked, and Mr. Kawalsky said that it was simple courtesy.

He handed me back the paper. "Show it to your father," he said. "Once he's read it, we'll both take it to Reverend Thanh."

Mom came to pick us up soon afterward, and as we drove home, I thought about my essay and about what Mr. Kawalsky had said about my writing. About my "gift" with words. What would Dad think about the essay, I wondered, and felt both excitement and apprehension.

When we got back to the house, I was still mulling over how and when to show the essay to Dad. I'd just about chickened out about showing it to him at all when there was the sound of a car roaring down Ferndale Road. Next minute, Dad's Ford Cutlass came screeching into the driveway. Brakes squealed

130

and Dad jumped out, slamming his door so hard it made a sound like a bomb exploding.

"What on *earth*?" Mom exclaimed.

We ran to the window and watched our father striding across our yard, pushing through the open space in the Blankards' privet fence, and marching over toward their house. As he did so, the Blankards' front door opened and Art came out on the porch.

Dad commenced hollering, but we couldn't hear a word. "Open the window," I told Mitch. He heaved it open and we hung out of the window in time to hear the end of what Dad was shouting.

"You have no honor," he bellowed. "I thought you were a friend of my family. Now I see you in your true colors."

Art Blankard had turned vermillion. He set his fists on his hips and roared back, "Listen, you jackass, don't you go talking to me about honor." Dad shouted, what did Art mean? "What do I mean? What do I *mean*? You were in with management when your sumbitching company closed that plant in our town," our neighbor hollered. "Where was your sumbitching honor then?"

Across the street, the Despards' door had opened a crack—in a second, Mrs. Despard was going to call the cops. Heedless of this possibility, Dad waved a newspaper under Art's nose. "So, that's why you did this despicable thing—to get back at me. Now I understand." He started to walk away, turned, and yelled, "Opportunist!"

"Crazy sumbitch!"

"*Bakayaro!*" Dad bellowed, and Mom turned and ran to the door, hauled it open, and raced down the driveway. Mitch and I watched, rooted to the ground, as Mom caught up to our dad, clasped both hands around his arm, and practically dragged him into the house.

"*Arré,*" Obaachan whispered, wide eyed. "*Arré, ma!* What has make Juntaro so angry?"

As soon as he hit the house, Dad threw a copy of one of those supermarket tabloids on the floor. He was beside himself, sputtering in English and Japanese, so I picked the newspaper up and read the headlines: "WE ALL LIVE IN FEAR."

Underneath the inch-tall headlines was a photo of the Blankards. The smaller caption read: "Mizuno neighbors tell of hell. Terrorized for living next to Asian family."

"Blankard sold this drivel to the tabloids," Dad seethed. "How could I have been so wrong about the man? *Asian* family—that moron!"

He stormed off to the kitchen and threw the paper in the trash. It bounced out, so he threw it in again. *"Bakayaro!"* he spluttered.

Dinner was not what you would call your everyday, happy meal. Dad was fuming. Mom tried to ease the mood with small talk, but the rest of us were stunned silent by the Blankards' betrayal. Finally, in desperation, Mom asked how Mr. Kawalsky was progressing in his new office.

"He liked Terri's essay," Mitch said.

It was an innocent comment, but right away, Dad's ears went back. "What essay?" he demanded.

Knowing that this was definitely *not* the time to show Dad my essay, I said that it was just something I'd written, nothing important. "Then why would you show it to the newspaper editor?" my father demanded. He pushed his uneaten dinner plate away and went, "Is there some reason you don't want to show this essay to me, Teresa?"

When my dad used my full name, I knew my back was to the wall. Wishing I'd thought to warn Mitch to keep quiet, I got my essay and handed it over silently.

As Dad started to read, some of the tension in his face seemed to drain away, and he looked older and thinner and tired to death. I watched him anxiously as he finished reading and then looked up at me.

"What are you going to do with this?" Dad asked

me. I told him what Mr. Kawalsky had suggested. "I don't think it's a good idea," he then said.

Well, so what else was new? I'd known from the start that my dad would never approve. Mitch, realizing he'd put his foot in it, started to backpedal.

"It's just Terri's opinion," he protested. "Anyway, Mr. Kawalsky says it reads pretty good."

"Reads pretty *well*. Your grammar is terrible." Dad set down the sheet of paper and rubbed his eyes. "The problem is that something like this could be seen as a weakness. It could damage our case against Waring."

He quit rubbing his eyes and looked at me. "Terri, I don't believe in that march, but I'm going along to show that the Mizunos are united as a family. What you write here could be interpreted to mean that you disagree with the rest of us."

"That's not the way I meant it," I said. I glanced at Mom, who had picked up the paper Dad set down and was reading it, then at Obaachan who was listening with a frown on her face. "You're twisting what I said," I protested.

Wrong move. Dad jumped all over me. If I had any sense, he lectured, I should be able to see that talk of peace and reconciliation and love would play right into Grace Fallister's hands. "She's the one who'll twist every word you've written," he told me. "She'll make it sound as if you think Waring isn't guilty."

He glowered at the trash can where he'd tossed the tabloid, and I knew what he was thinking. With our next-door neighbors feeling that we're a threat to their safety, the Mizunos needed to stand tough and stand together.

Mom nodded unhappily. "I agree with your father. That Fallister person could use your essay to hurt us in court."

As I got up to start carrying dishes to the kitchen, I told myself that no way did I want Ms. Fallister to profit by what I'd written. Dad was right, and that

133

was the end of it. There was no earthly reason why I should feel hurt.

When I'd finished the dishes and gone upstairs to my room, the first thing I did was to crumple up my essay. I was about to throw it into the trash can under my desk when the door behind me opened.

"*Arré*—don't throw away," Obaachan scolded. "I want to read."

She snagged the paper from my surprised hand and held it to the light. Oh, why not? I thought. One more negative comment wasn't going to kill me.

I was getting into my homework when Obaachan spoke again. "You write all by yourself?" I nodded. "Very good written," Obaachan then said. "You clever girl."

My grandmother was praising me? Me, the klutz, the non-picker-upper of clothes, the most *shikataganai* of her grandchildren, who would never get a Japanese (or any other kind of) husband? I gaped at her as she carefully settled herself on her bed.

"Is true," she said. And then she said something I couldn't understand. "It is old Japanese proverb," she informed me. "It say, 'Man's life is only a candle in the wind.'" She paused. "You are right, Terri-chan, and Juntaro is wrong."

Obaachan admitting Dad could be wrong? Totally blown away, I listened as she went on, "Hate from inside a person is what put the candle out. Biggest enemy is inside a man, not outside him."

I could relate to that. "Hate can kill," I agreed.

"Worse than that," Obaachan struggled with words, trying them out on her tongue and rejecting them before she went on, "hating can kill the person who hates."

Downstairs, I could hear Mom's and Mitch's voices, the background noise of the TV. "Are you talking about Dad?" I asked Obaachan, and when she didn't answer, I suddenly had this irrational need to defend him. "Listen, he never acted like this before. What happened to Harris has made us all a little nuts."

Obaachan ignored me. "Juntaro was the only boy who lived," she murmured.

Even more surprised, I sat back at my desk and listened. "First Mariko-chan is born, and then two sons die soon after they are born. I pray every day to Lady Kwannon, and when she cannot hear me I prayed to Maria-sama of the Christian church. I begged to ancestors, too," Obaachan added, "and maybe they listen because Juntaro was born. He lived! His father love him best in world."

I gazed at the stern-looking man framed on Obaachan's spirit altar and tried to imagine him loving anyone. I couldn't, but Obaachan was still talking, so I paid attention.

All along I'd known that Japanese men doted on their firstborn sons—I mean, I'd seen Dad with Harris for fifteen years. But what I hadn't realized was that Dad was a marshmallow compared to my grandfather Mizuno. That old guy ran his family like a military academy. Still, according to Obaachan, nothing was too good for little Juntaro. Toys, clothes, food—and education. He had it all.

"What about Aunt Mariko?" I asked. Obaachan looked surprised.

"She is girl," she reminded me. "In Japan, men comes first. When I was child, Mama teach me women are born to make men comfortable."

Chewing on that grizzly bit of information, I realized I hadn't appreciated Mom enough. Supposing Alice and I had been born in Japan? The horror of this thought increased as I listened to my Japanese grandmother explaining how she'd sat up many a night waiting for her high-living husband to come home from a night out with the boys. He was usually very late, but what did Obaachan do while waiting for Grandfather Mizuno to stroll through the door?

"I mend clothes for family. Later, Mariko sometimes keep me company. Good training for her."

Some training. Listening to how my grandmother had taught Mariko to get up earlier than the servants, how she'd taught her how to prepare *wakame* soup each morning and boil rice without burning it—it made my blood run cold.

"Someday, I know she thank me." I guess my mouth was hanging open because Obaachan added sternly, "Thank me when she marry. Girls must be train to be good wives."

"Didn't boys have to get up early, too?" I asked, but the sarcasm was lost on her.

"Oh, yes," she said, very serious. "In Japan, boys must be strong like north wind. Each morning, my husband and Juntaro practice *ken-dō*. You know what that is?"

When I was little, Dad had used to play around with a wooden sword in the backyard early Sunday morning before the neighbors got up. "*Ken-dō* good for the spirit," Obaachan assured me. "Make boy grow strong with pure spirit."

But I didn't care about that. I was thinking of Mariko sweating over *wakame* soup and burning her little fingers on rice. "Things have changed, right?" I asked, hopefully, and Obaachan heaved a sigh that seemed to come from the soles of her feet.

"Everything change when war start."

Apparently the Second World War had scuttled my grandfather's hopes of teaching little Juntaro the way of the pure spirit. When Dad was still a little kid, Grandfather Mizuno had been sent to fight in the Coral Sea.

"I never forget the day he sail—blue skies, and big white ship," Obaachan said, her eyes far away and remembering. "Mariko and Jun-chan and I—we so proud."

She stopped talking and looked down at her wrinkled hands. "What happened?" I finally asked.

In a few spare words she sketched what a real war had been like, and all the old John Wayne movies with the blood and guts, honor and glory disappeared from my mind forever. Obaachan and her kids had faced growing hunger and bombing raids that came by day and by night, bombs that turned homes into firetraps and neighbors into charred corpses.

"Our house in Osaka bombed in 1943," she related calmly. "We lucky to escape, because next-door neighbors buried under falling house. But now, there was problem. Where shall we go?"

Luckily, Grandfather Mizuno had a cousin in the country. Obaachan and her little ones traveled eighty miles—by rail and on foot—to reach the small town of Obayama. Not so luckily, Grandpa's cousin was a mean man who begrudged every grain of rice. Obaachan had to scrub floors and work in the cousin's back garden harvesting potatoes till her fingers were bleeding raw. "Not so bad, though," my grandmother pointed out. "We eat."

But, then, disaster came. A letter had come saying Grandfather Mizuno had been killed in action.

"*Killed?* But—but didn't he come back from the war? I thought—"

"Wait," Obaachan directed.

The battleship on which Grandfather Mizuno served had been sunk by the Americans, and Obaachan had received notification that her husband had died fighting gloriously for his country. The cousin promptly threw my grandmother and the kids out.

Now *that* was a real prince. I said a few things about that slimy cousin, and Obaachan put her hand over her mouth to hide a chuckle.

"Your voice just now exactly like your papa, Terri-chan." She said, "You too much like him."

I said, true, I was tall like Dad. "No, not just looking like. In other ways, in spirit and heart." She put a small hand to her chest. "You feel things *here*.

137

Juntaro, too. When he was boy, he write poetry. You don't know this?"

Dad a poet? But Obaachan had already resumed her story.

She spoke of begging for food by the road, even stealing vegetables to feed her kids. Eventually, the small family drifted back to Osaka, where Obaachan hoped to find work of some kind.

"It was better, there, right?" I pleaded.

"Worse, worse! City is sea of flame. We run here—we run there. Always, people running. Always, people hungry, people sick! Then Japan surrender and Americans are coming. We are told terrible devil Americans will kill our chirrun."

I had to laugh at Obaachan's description of Americans, but she was in deadly earnest. "They say *gaijin* have big noses, like devils. *Blue* eyes, if you can believe! People tell us, American soldier eat babies."

I asked, so did she run away? Obaachan spread her arms as if to say, where could we go? "The day the Americans come into Osaka, I take chirrun by hand and stand on road and look at jeeps coming. I think—if they kill us, they kill us all together. Juntaro—"

Obaachan stopped, lifted suddenly shaking fingers to her lips. "Juntaro pull away from me and run into street. Almost run in front of jeep. He yell at bad men who killed his father. One of the soldier got out, pick Jun-chan up—"

She stopped in midsentence and looked at me with eyes that, across the years, still held a look of disbelief. "Soldier not angry, you can believe? Give us cracker, chocolate." Obaachan looked down at her tightly clasped hands. "If I am strong, proud woman, I would tell chirrun, throw away this American food. But they are hungry, so, I take the candy and exchange on black market for rice."

Under the occupation, life eased a little. Obaachan found work as a servant for an American family. She

I walked along Ferndale, we saw a black Toyota parked on the other side of the road. "Isn't that Damon Ying and his cousin?" Kawalsky wondered. "Do they live around here?"

I said I didn't think so. "Maybe they're picking up a friend," I added.

Nick just nodded. Then he asked, really casual, "Have you talked to Damon lately?" I shook my head, and he went, "Oh," and then got quiet.

" 'Oh,' what?" I asked. The memory of that scene in the park gave my words a rough edge, so I softened it. "Damon was Harris's friend, not mine. He's a senior, remember? He hasn't even been *in* school since senior finals."

"I was just thinking—" Kawalsky hesitated another beat and then changed the subject. "You heard about the new movie playing at the Crystal Showcase?" I shook my head, puzzled by this rapid shift. "Kids who saw it say it's pretty funny. We could do with a few laughs, right?"

For sure, I said. In fact, I didn't know when I'd laughed last. Kawalsky didn't say anything but looked at me expectantly, and it suddenly hit me that he'd just asked me out on a date.

It blew my mind. I mean, Nick was my *friend*. My good friend. In fact, if the truth be told, I was closer to Kawalsky than to anyone because not even to Melanie in the old days, not even to Alice or Mitch, would I have told the secret of my meeting Waring in the park.

But no matter how I valued Nick's good qualities, he didn't come close to making me feel the way I did when Damon even glanced my way.

"Maybe it's not such a good idea," Nick was saying. His voice was carefully cheerful, which, because I knew him so well, meant he was feeling hurt and let down.

Way to go, Terri, I snarled at myself. Now I'd hurt my friend—but my thought trailed off as Nick

141

reached out and caught hold of my shoulder. He gave it a little shake. "It's *okay*," he told me. "It was just an idea. There'll be other movies."

"Sure," I said, feeling miserable.

"The thing is, we've got to get through this march and then the trial," Kawalsky went on, changing the subject once again. "After that, the Society of Aryan Warriors will pull out of here and go back to Louisiana, and the so-called SAW will crawl back under their rocks. Maybe we'll even be able to get back to normal."

Ahead of us, Mitch was romping down the street with Walker, and I envied him. Even with all the trouble around us, Mitch could still be carefree. "I don't know if we'll ever get back to normal," I was beginning, when Nick stopped me.

"Listen," he hissed. I held my breath. "No—I guess it was nothing."

"What?" I asked. "Don't do this to me, Kawalsky. What did you hear?"

"I thought—" He broke off, and I could see Nick stiffen up, listening. Then he said, "It's nothing. Probably just the wind."

We kept on walking. Ahead of us, Mitch was bawling Walker out for finding a half-full box of pizza in a trash can. "Yech," Mitch said, "quit that, Walker. You want to get worms?"

And then I heard the sound, too. Clear as moonlight, I'd heard a shoe scrape on the pavement. I whipped around to see what was behind me, but there was nobody in sight.

"Somebody's playing stupid games," Nick gritted. "C'mon, we'll go over to the convenience store and call your house from there."

Wenstein's was still a couple of blocks away. "Let's go faster," I suggested.

Just then Walker turned and growled. I jerked my head over my shoulder and had time to glimpse shadowy figures following us. Man-sized shadows—four of them.

Then I heard Nick yell, "Terri—run!" And then, they were on us.

TEN

BEFORE I COULD run, before I could even scream, a rough hand grabbed me by the hair and yanked back my head. "Don't make a sound, bitch," warned a muffled voice, "or you'll be sorry."

A white-hooded face hung directly above me, a demon's featureless face, with slits for one blue eye and one brown eye. I tried to yell again, but Karo jerked my neck further back and sound was strangled into my throat.

"I said, shut your mouth," he snarled. Then he slapped me.

Ears, cheeks, teeth, and eyes stinging from that blow, I still heard a commotion going on nearby—Walker barking and snarling and Kawalsky's muffled voice shouting, "Let go of her, you—"

There came a yell of real pain. I tried again to twist free, but Karo gave me no slack. Pain stabbed through my face into my stretched-tight throat until I was sure that my neck would snap. Then came a shouted curse, a canine yowl of pain.

"Goddamned hound," someone raged.

Karo slugged me again. Then I heard him snap, "Car coming—okay, we're *out* of here."

The punishing grip on my hair loosened so suddenly that I fell backward onto the hard pavement.

"Oww—" But the moan of pain didn't come from me. Kawalsky lay crumpled near me.

"Nick!" I shrieked. Another moan. He was alive anyway. And Mitch? Where was—

"You okay, Walker, you okay?"

Twenty feet away, my little brother was sitting up and sobbing. His arms were wrapped around Walker, who was whining and licking Mitch's face. I called to him, but he didn't hear me.

Anyway, he was okay. I switched my attention back to Nick, who didn't look okay at all. He was mounded up in a fetal position, his arms tucked into his belly. His glasses were broken, and his nose was bleeding.

"You're hurt," I wailed. "I'll go get someone—"

I looked up hopefully as a car whooshed past us, going fast. It didn't slow down. "Don't go—alone—they may be still—around," Nick was gritting. Then he asked, "Did they hurt you, Terri?"

I said no, I was more scared than anything else, which was true. Up till now things had moved so quickly I hadn't had time to feel scared. Now, terror at what might have happened brought shivers I couldn't control. I tried to keep my teeth from chattering as Kawalsky tucked his face back into his chest and cradled his stomach.

"I'm okay," he mumbled. "Just got the wind kicked out of me."

Just then Mitch came hobbling toward us. His right eye was raising a shiner, and he had a bloody lip. Next to him Walker limped along on three feet. "They were gonna beat me up, but Walker bit the guy who was holding me," Mitch babbled. "Walker took a big bite out of his arm, and then that jerk kicked Walker and hurt his leg." He paused to gulp breath. "Terri, your face is all red. Nick, you okay?"

I said I was going for help. "Stay with him, and I'll run down to that house over there and knock on the door—"

"No," Nick and Mitch both said, and when what I was saying hit me, I dried up. "We have to stick together," Kawalsky insisted.

He took a deep breath and got to his knees, whereupon Mitch and I each grabbed him by an arm and

145

hauled him to his feet. "Let's go to Wenstein's," Nick croaked. "It's not far."

"Those creeps may still be around," I cautioned, and Mitch snarled that he surely hoped so.

"I want to get my hands on that sumbitch that hurt Walker," he growled.

It hit me funny that Mitch had used Art Blankard's pet expression at such a time. Funny, peculiar, I mean, there really being nothing humorous about what had happened—except maybe the pop-eyed look Mr. Wenstein gave us when we all hobbled into his store.

Mr. Wenstein called the cops and our folks. Apparently Mr. Kawalsky had just left our house seconds before, but the Mizuno parents arrived in about two minutes. They'd just quit making sure we were okay when the sirens came wailing down the street.

"I'm getting to hate that sound," Mitch sighed.

The officer in charge was Sergeant Gady, who'd been on the scene when the *Herald* office went up in flames. She asked if we'd recognized our assailants.

"It was Karo," I said and explained about his peculiar eyes. My fear was ebbing away, and what I most felt was mad. How dared Karo and his goons attack us on our own street in our own hometown?

"And Walker took a chunk out of one of them!" Mitch cut in. "Walker kept me from being beaten up."

Mom eyed Walker in a way that promised him steaks for a month. "You'll arrest these criminals?" Dad wanted to know.

Sergeant Gady said that an APB had been issued and requested that we come down to headquarters to make our statements. Dad wasn't about to let us out of his sight, so the three of us, plus Walker, jammed into the back of our car.

On the ride over, Dad was riding a short fuse. "They must have been waiting for you," he seethed. "Lying in wait and watching for my children." He slammed his hand into the steering wheel and Mom said, Jun, for God's sake, be careful. "I'd like ten minutes with Karo," he snarled. "Ten minutes alone."

Mitch said Walker had helped to even the score. In spite of his bruises, he sounded excited. Kawalsky, on the other hand, was so quiet that I worried about him. "You okay?" I whispered.

"Yeah—just spinning a thread," he said. That was all, but he winced when we got out of the car at the police station, and I saw him touch his stomach. Mom saw it, too.

"You need to see a doctor, Nick," she exclaimed. "I *wish* your father had stayed—he said he had to check on something downtown and would come right back to fetch you." She smoothed Nick's hair back from his eyes, adding worriedly, "Jun, never mind statements to the police—we need to take Nick to Xavier."

Kawalsky said, no, he was fine, all he wanted was to make his statement and go home. In proof of this he limp-led us up the police-station steps and inside the swinging doors. "Can I call my father again?" he asked.

I waited with him while he made his call. "He's still not home—and he's not answering his car phone, either, so I just left a message on his machine." Nick paused, said, "Terri—" and stopped again.

"What?" I prodded.

"It—well, it just struck me funny. You remember seeing Damon and his cousin in that parked car? They were parked on Ferndale, right?"

Before I could respond, the swinging doors of the station house were pushed inward, and Damon and Jerry Cho came in shoving two white men ahead of them. One of them was a chunky, bald-shaven guy with one blue eye and one brown.

"What the hell is going on?" Sergeant Gady exclaimed while at the same time, Mitch whistled and called, "Hey, Damon, way to go!"

Damon Ying had his prisoner in a hammerlock. The

guy had a jagged, bleeding wound in his arm, and, from the look on his face, was in severe pain.

"Recognize this scum without his mask, Mitch?" Damon crowed. Excitement made his eyes glow, and he flashed his touchdown grin at us. His prisoner cursed violently. "Keep your mouth shut, or I'll close it for you," Damon warned.

An inner-office door opened, and Police Chief Brandon came out. Even before he could ask what was happening, Jerry Cho said, "We've found these perps for you, Chief."

He gave Karo's arm a twist. "These *gentlemen* are members of the Brotherhood of SAW. The local branch of the noble Society of Aryan Warriors. A half hour ago, they and two of their pals were brave enough to beat up three kids. The other two got away from us, but I doubt if they'll get too far."

Chief Brandon opened his mouth, but once more got intercepted as Karo spit out a dozen curses. "He's lying, the gook freak," he bellowed. "We're walking peacefully along, and these slopes attack us for no reason. We're going to sue your ass for this, you mongreloid—"

He broke off in a yell of pain as Jerry Cho wrenched his arm back. "See how it feels," Jerry snarled. "This is what you did to those kids. Must've made you feel *proud.*"

Chief Brandon finally got a word in edgewise. "Sergeant Gady, take charge of these suspects. Mr. Cho—in my office, please."

"No, let's do this out here," Jerry Cho said. His upper lip curled as he added in a loud voice, "I want everyone—especially the kids who were hurt tonight—to see how tough these *warriors* really are. We caught up to them a mile or so past Wenstein's, boasting about what they'd done. That is, three of them were boasting. One of them was in tears because one of the kids' dogs bit him."

"He's the one who kicked Walker," Mitch glowered.

The police chief told his staring officers to get the creeps out of his sight. "Hold them on suspicion of assault," he directed.

"*Suspicion?*" Dad repeated incredulously, as Karo and his pals were hustled out. "But you heard what happened. They were boasting of hurting my children."

"Suspicion. By law they're innocent till proven guilty." The chief turned to Jerry and Damon. "You won't mind my asking—just what were you two doing in that area of town?"

"Why are you questioning these men?" Dad demanded. "They aren't criminals. Those men who hurt my children are the criminals."

As if he were taking inventory, he tilted Mitch's face up, ran a thumb over the beginning of a black eye. He reached out, and I winced as I felt him trace my hurt cheek. "Is that painful?" he asked me.

I shook my head, but he'd already swung around to Jerry. "I have to thank you, Mr. Cho," he said formally. "I'm in your debt."

Jerry Cho just shrugged. "These scum don't care which rules they break, Mr. Mizuno. They thumb their noses at the police, so we made a citizen's arrest. Now we'd better hope the cops can manage to hold onto these bums and arrest their friends, too."

"They had better." Dad wheeled around to face Chief Brandon. "If not, I'll take matters into my own hands."

In that moment he looked ready to take on the entire Brotherhood of SAW. "No one hurts my children," Dad added.

Chief Brandon looked tired. "You don't think I know how you feel? I have kids, too, Mr. Mizuno. Take your family home and let us do our job."

"As long as you *do* your job," Jerry needled. "When was the last time you did that?"

A slow red burned into Chief Brandon's face, and I

heard Sergeant Gady mutter something about it hitting the fan.

"How many crimes against Asians have you solved?" Jerry demanded. "How many perps have served time for what they've done?"

"I suppose your so-called Asian Power Through Unity group does better?" snapped Chief Brandon. Leveling a finger at Jerry he added, "I know all about you, Cho, and I'm warning you. Start trouble around here, and you'll be sorry."

"We don't *cause* the trouble." Jerry Cho paused, and his eyes became dark and deadly. "If trouble comes looking for us, that's another story."

The whole police station was listening. "Get him *out* of here," the chief snapped, turned on his heel, and slammed into his office.

Jerry Cho raised both hands, palms outward, and backed out of the swinging doors. Damon followed, with a wink at Mitch. Me, he totally ignored.

Dad followed them, and we hurried after him. "Jun," Mom pleaded, "let's get the kids home. Nick needs to see a doctor. Jun," she exclaimed, as Dad turned away from us and began walking toward Damon and Jerry. "*Please*, let's just go home."

As if he hadn't heard a thing Mom had said, Dad continued to walk. She clenched her hands into fists. "Don't *do* this to me," she wailed. "Don't shut me out, Jun Mizuno. I lost a son, too."

Completely ignoring her, our father joined Jerry and Damon. I watched him shake their hands and settle down to talk while beside me Nick gnawed his lower lip.

Mom took several deep breaths, and then told us to get into the car. As we were about to climb into the backseat, Mr. Kawalsky's van came barreling up.

Nick looked relieved. "I'd better get over there—it'll take him forever to climb out of the van."

He started toward the van, and I followed him. "Is something bugging you?" Nick said nothing. "You didn't finish what you were going to say before—about Damon and Jerry," I prodded.

"It just seemed strange is all," Kawalsky muttered. I asked, what was strange, for Pete's sake? "Karo and his buddies came down Ferndale after us. They'd have had to pass Jerry's parked car, right? So how come Jerry and Damon didn't try to stop them—or at least, follow them?"

It took a second for what Kawalsky was suggesting to register. "Maybe they didn't see that we were being followed," I protested.

"Could be. But there's another thing, Terri. The car that passed us after we were beaten up was a *black* car. I didn't see if it was a Toyota or not, though."

"You think those two set us up?" Nick said nothing. "You really think Damon and Jerry Cho *wanted* us to be beaten up? *Why* would they want a sick thing like that?"

"Well, if you figure it out—"

"Nick!" Mr. Kawalsky had succeeded in climbing out of the van and was now hobbling toward us hollering, "You hurt, son? Are you all right?"

Kawalsky started limping toward his father. As I turned back to walk to our car, I noted that Dad was still talking with Jerry.

Why *hadn't* Damon and his cousin stopped Karo from hurting us? I asked myself, and the answer was that it didn't make any sense. *Figure it out*, Nick had said, and I set out to reason it out methodically, the way he always did.

First point: Jerry Cho hated and despised the Brotherhood of SAW. He was also busy getting together a group like the one he'd led in L.A. But perhaps the new APU league wasn't forming quickly enough, or it wasn't as committed as Jerry wanted it to be.

Could it be that Jerry had *wanted* an incident like our being beaten to spark an explosion of rage and swell the ranks of his group?

"Maybe," I muttered aloud.

Second point: Why had Jerry and Damon been parked on Ferndale Road to start with? Had they seen Karo and his friends driving out toward our street and followed them?

If so, Jerry and Damon had to know there'd be trouble. They must have seen Karo and his buddies follow us. Yet, instead of acting to protect us, they'd waited, maybe even cold-bloodedly watched while we were being beaten up. Then they'd driven right by us to find the skinheads and make their citizen's arrest.

Third point, and the kicker: Supposing Jerry's anger at the incident caught hold amongst his followers. Wouldn't that raw, red-hot, unthinking fury be something he could use to physically crush the hated Brotherhood of SAW?

For a second I played with these thoughts—then backed off. I didn't want to remember the look in Dad's eye when he walked over to Jerry and Damon. I didn't want to believe that Dad might be a new recruit for Jerry's private army.

"No," Dad said flatly. "I won't change my mind. If Cho and his group aren't allowed to march tomorrow, neither will we."

Perched on one of our living-room chairs, his long face even longer, Rev. Thanh looked like a mournful heron. "But, Mr. Mizuno," he argued, "I don't believe you understand the ramifications. After the, ah, beating incident occurred, Cho's Asian Power Through Unity group has swelled to more than fifty members."

"Right on," Mitch muttered.

I glanced at Mom, sitting on the living-room couch. Her forehead was puckered into a frown of concentration as Rev. Thanh went on, "Don't you see that their presence would turn our march into a—a dangerous confrontation with the supremacists?"

"There'll be no danger if the SAW keeps its dis-

152

tance." My father folded his arms across his chest in a gesture that said, don't mess with me.

Rev. Thanh's Adam's apple bobbed up and down in agitation. "Mr. Mizuno," he pleaded, "the purpose of this march is to show that the Asian Advancement Group *rejects* the violence that caused your son's death. It's a peaceful march, Mr. Mizuno, and Jerry Cho *wants* violence."

Dad didn't say a word, but I saw that his hands were clenched hard as if he had a grip on someone's throat and wasn't about to let go. "Read what it says here." Rev. Thanh waved a hand-out sheet under Dad's nose. "Just read!"

Dad sat down on the couch so that Mom could read, too, and Mitch and I peered over their shoulders. In inch-high black letters, the sheet of paper questioned: "HAVEN'T WE HAD ENOUGH?" Beneath this there was a graphic photograph of an Asian boy lying on the street, spread-eagled, slack-jawed, his chest a bloody mess. The caption under the photo declared, "Murdered by Hate" and was followed by a list of crimes that the Society of Aryan Warriors had allegedly committed throughout the country.

"Most recently, two Asian youngsters were beaten up in Westriver by local white supremacists," the leaflet concluded. "Are we or are we not Americans? Do we have the right to protect our own against mad-dog racists? Do we have the right to defend ourselves, as the Constitution states?"

Beside me, Mitch repeated, "Right on!"

His eyes were hard, and he looked every bit as fierce as Dad. Rev. Thanh pleaded, "Nobody hates bigotry more than I do, but what Cho wants to do is wrong. Besides, I'm not sure that Senator Buford will participate in our march if there's a threat of violence."

"Then do without the senator." Dad handed Rev. Thanh back the flyer, adding curtly, "I agree with Cho. We've got the right to protect our own."

153

"These white supremacists are such terrible people," Mom added. Her eyes were far away, and I knew that reading about all that violence and bloodshed had triggered memories with which she couldn't cope.

The reverend knew he was fighting a losing battle. "If I could cancel the march, I would," he sighed. "But there's no turning back. We have Asian groups and sympathizers from Vermont, Maine, and from as far off as New Jersey. We have nearly three thousand people marching to show support for you, Mr. Mizuno."

He rattled off a list of organizations that were going to march. "You think they will march with Cho's vigilantes? Please, please be reasonable."

"Reasonable!" Like a stretched-tight rubber band, Dad snapped to his feet and confronted Rev. Thanh. "Reason doesn't work. Justice is a freak show with everybody out for himself, and that includes your precious Senator Buford. *You* want publicity for your Asian coalition, Reverend. You want numbers. Well, you won't have them without the Mizunos, and my family doesn't march without Jerry Cho."

He meant what he said, and Rev. Thanh knew it. He gave up, spoke in a subdued voice telling us that we were to meet at eight o'clock, sharp, at the Boston Common, and left the house.

Our father walked the reverend to his car. He moved with a raw energy, his eyes were bright, and he even whistled under his breath. But the cold fire that burned him made my skin prickle with uneasiness. This wasn't the father I knew.

"Way to go, Dad," Mitch muttered, and my tension level went still higher. Since the night we got beaten up, Mitch had changed, too. Eyes snapping with excitement he crowed, *"Now* we'll have a real march."

He ran out in the back to commune with Walker. Mom seemed to shake herself awake. "Terri," she said, "see if your grandmother needs anything."

All this time, Obaachan had been upstairs ringing

her bell and saying her prayers. I went to our shared room and found her kneeling by her spirit altar. When she saw me, she patted the floor beside her.

"What did Reverend Thanh say?" she asked and, when I'd explained, added, "You are marching?"

"All of us are. Alice is coming home tonight to march with the family. How about you, Obaachan?"

She gave a small shake of her white head. "There'll be buses coming from all over the state with lots and lots of people. There'll be music and marching bands, all in Harris's honor."

I was talking cheerfully but even before I'd finished talking, Obaachan was shaking her head. "Why not?" I asked.

"It is frightening," Obaachan replied. She then said it in Japanese, not using the word *kowai*, which meant scary, but *osoroshii*, which my growing number of Japanese words told me meant terrifying. I thought that she meant that she'd overheard something about Jerry Cho making trouble and tried to reassure her—and myself.

"There'll be cops all along the way for crowd control," I said. "They won't let any trouble start. Jerry Cho's APU group is just going to march to show sympathy for the rest of us."

"APU, SAW—I not remembering any of those silly names," Obaachan said fretfully. She put down her little spirit bell and sat looking at the framed photographs on Alice's desk.

For a second I thought she was praying quietly, to herself, but then all of a sudden she said, "It happens again."

"What?" I asked, bewildered.

"All bad thing," Obaachan told me sadly. "Terri-chan, when your grandfather come back from war, he is too much sick and bitter. He was in prisoner-of-war camp. This is great dishonor for Japanese. He feel Americans dishonor him, so he hate Americans!"

Grandfather Mizuno had made Obaachan quit her

job, even if that was the only money coming into the family. They'd nearly starved all over again until Grandfather finally got work teaching history at a local high school.

"He hate Americans," Obaachan repeated sadly. "Years pass, and he hate more and more. So much he hate that Juntaro becomes curious about these terrible people. Secretly, he study English."

Obaachan shook her head over such unthinkable rebellion. "When he is in the high school, Juntaro meet American teacher who offer him chance to go to college in America. On scholarship."

This much of the story I knew—sort of. Dad had said he was really excited at the opportunity, the wonderful adventure of coming to a new country. "What did Grandfather Mizuno say?" I asked Obaachan now, and she sighed.

"He say to Juntaro, if you go, you don't come back," Obaachan replied sadly. "He say, if you go, you are dead to me. Mariko take father's side. She and Juntaro have terrible fight."

But Dad really wanted to try his wings. He was sure that he'd go back to Japan and patch things up with his father and sister, but while he was at college he'd met Mom and decided to become an American citizen. Grandfather Mizuno had never mentioned Dad's name again, and neither had Mariko.

"As much as he loves before, now he hates his son." Obaachan wiped her eyes on the back of her hand. "So sad, Terri-chan. At the bottom of my husband's heart, he suffer too bad because he truly love his son. I see this in husband's eyes every day. Before he die, I beg him, don't die with this anger in your heart. Tell me you forgive our son. He say, 'I have no son. All my sons are dead.'"

Two tears oozed out of her eyes and began to trail down her crisscrossed cheeks. "I'm sorry," I whispered. It was all I could think of to say.

"All these long years, I do not see my son."

Obaachan wept. The sobs seemed to tear her bony chest and, hardly thinking, I put my arms around her. She seemed all dry bones, small and light, as she leaned into my hug. On my shoulder, I felt the burn of her hot tears and knew that my own eyes were brimming.

"You wrote to us." I tried to console her. "Every year, you wrote."

"*He* did not know I write. I disobey my husband," my grandmother mourned. "But how can I pretend my Jun-chan is dead? How?" She gave a terrible, dry sob. "For more than twenty years, I don't see my son, not see grandchirren. Never see Harrisu."

I rubbed her bone-thin back but couldn't think of a thing to say to comfort her. And then, she said it. "Terri-chan," she told me, "I come to America because I afraid to die without knowing my son's chirrun. Now, I sorry I came."

"Why?" I whispered. "Why, Obaachan?"

She pushed away from my hug and peered intently at me with tear-red old eyes. "Juntaro now growing more like his father all time. I afraid too much of what going to happen now, Terri-chan. I *afraid*."

ELEVEN

"WHAT THIS REMINDS me of is a Fourth-of-July parade," Alice said. "Nothing scary here, so quit being such a fraidy cat, Terriyaki."

Though she tried to sound her usual flip self, Alice looked tired. "What?" she demanded, when she caught me staring. I told her the bags under her eyes had bags, and she quipped, "So maybe I've found a new boyfriend."

"Have you?" Alice gave me a look that said, who do you think you're dealing with? "Anybody special?" I prodded.

"We-e-ll—" Alice attempted a knowing smile, then gave it up. "Not really. Look, I *didn't* want to come here today, but Dad made it sound like, be here or else. I wish the march was over."

"I wish the whole thing was over," I muttered, and Alice pointed out that everybody else seemed to be having a good time.

The dozen buses parked on Charles Street had brought a gazillion people. Most of these milled around the speakers' platform that had been set up earlier, or in the part of the Common nearest the corner of Charles and Beacon Streets where the march was going to begin. The Westriver Junior-Senior High marching band was practicing not far from us, and Ms. Sophie Ziegler, a zaftig new-age singer who was the rage in Boston, was schmoozing with her band.

In the midst of this Rev. Thanh and his assistants

ran around organizing, answering questions, directing groups according to a master plan they'd drafted.

The group marching against the use of handguns went *here*, the antiviolence group went *there*, and the Asian group from New Hampshire was to march right after the African Americans Against Racism. Connecticut marchers went there, the delegation from Rhode Island followed the New Yorkers, and Vermonters mingled with the handful of Canadians who'd come down from Montreal and Toronto to help the cause.

"Not that it matters a whole bunch, but where do *we* march?" Alice wondered as we watched stragglers being rounded up and maneuvered into place.

Rev. Thanh had put the Mizunos up front, right behind the clergy representing all the major religions. "In case God is listening, Reverend Thanh isn't taking any chances," my irrepressible sister joked. "So where's the handsome Senator Buford going to be? Next to me, I hope."

I explained that Mom, Dad, and the senator were to march behind the clergy, and we kids would follow just behind them. Alice started to comment, then broke off to click her tongue. "Mom's calling us. She shouldn't wear black—it makes her look sallow."

It had been Rev. Thanh's idea that all of us wear mourning, so Mom had put on the suit she wore at Harris's funeral. She'd lost weight since April, and it hung on her awkwardly. She looked as if she'd aged ten years in two months.

"Have you seen your father?" she asked distractedly when we came up. "He and Mitch wandered off somewhere. What a lot of people! I'm so glad your grandmother decided not to come—it would've been much too much for her."

Just then Rev. Thanh bustled up. "It's time to take your places," he told us. "Where's the rest of the family?"

While he was talking, I'd spotted Dad and my little

brother. They were surrounded by a group of people, mostly Asian, mostly male, almost all young. Each of these people wore a black arm band.

"Jerry Cho's Asian Power Through Unity group," the reverend said sourly. "They've been handing out those inflammatory leaflets to all the marchers."

I spotted Damon in the group around my dad and brother, but there was no sign of Jerry. Alice nudged me. "I'll bet Mitch wishes he could march with them," she said. "Look at his face."

Mitch's expression mirrored the excitement of Jerry's followers. In uneasy silence I watched as Rev. Thanh crossed over to talk to Dad. "Can't say's I blame him, especially after what happened to you guys," Alice went on.

"It's time the racist freaks got the fight they want." Damon's voice rose above the noise and babble. "As Jerry says, we don't want to start anything, but we'll sure finish it."

A murmur of agreement rose from the APU, and both my father and brother nodded. Mom bit her lower lip. "I hope this march isn't a mistake," she said nervously.

Mom had dark lines under her eyes, too, and her face was puffy, as if she'd cried all night. Impulsively, I put an arm around her waist. "It'll be okay," I whispered.

Absently, she patted my hand. "I keep reminding myself that it's for Harris," she said, and her eyes went suddenly bleak and empty, as if she were trying to look down into herself for my big brother and couldn't find him. It made me want to cry. Mom, I wanted to tell her, I know what you're feeling.

But now wasn't the time. Rev. Thanh collected Dad and Mitch and ushered us up the long line of marchers so that we could take our place behind the line of clergy. Standing there we listened as Rev. Thanh picked up his bullhorn and addressed us.

"Okay, people," he announced, "today's the day we've been waiting for. Isn't it a fabulous morning?"

Voices shouted enthusiastic response. "You'll see our schedule on your handout sheets. We'll exit the Common right here and walk down Charles on our first leg of the march. We'll walk around the Common three times, then stop at the speakers' platform. We clergy, the Mizuno family, Senator Buford, and the other speakers will take their seats on the platform."

He made a broad gesture toward us as if to say here are the mourners, folks, the reason why we're here, and there was a polite ripple of acknowledgment and sympathy. Then the reverend went on to add that Senator Buford would deliver the keynote address and that he wanted to say a special thank you to the Westriver Junior-Senior High School marching band and to Sophie Ziegler, who'd kindly volunteered to sing for us. Ms. Ziegler blew kisses at the enthusiastic crowd.

"After the music and speeches," Rev. Thanh resumed, "the Mizunos, Senator Buford, and we clergy will walk up the stone stairs directly behind the speakers' platform, cross Beacon Street, and climb up the State House steps to present a petition to the governor."

The reverend looked around at all of us. "That document affirms the need for understanding between peoples," he said, and his beautiful deep voice danced and rolled over us like a velvet river. "That document decries *any* act of violence."

Subtle the reverend wasn't. Unfortunately, his words fell on absent ears—there was still no sign of Jerry Cho. The media was well represented though. News wagons and TV trucks with cameras were all around us filming the various groups of marchers.

And there were so many groups. The Asian Advancement Group held blown-up photos of Harris and signs calling for justice and social reform. The antihandgun group declared that yes, guns *did* kill.

161

There were signs asking for peace, brotherhood, and tolerance mingling with signs with Senator Buford's face and the caption, "Buford Stands for Change." There were individual marchers, not affiliated with any group but just there to show support. There were even members of a religious community, all dressed up in white, who marched under a flag that showed a golden circle.

"Those people belong to the Sacred Circle." I hadn't heard Nick come up to us. I envied him—he looked cool and comfortable in shorts and a baggy T-shirt.

"A cult?" I asked.

"What's a cult, anyway? People who believe in something," Kawalsky said, reasonable as always. "The Circlists believe that what happened to Harris was wrong."

The bruises had faded from Nick's face, but there was a crooked tilt to his nose, which had been broken and reset. I felt hatred stir in me, welcomed it. It was a lot easier to hate Karo and his mentally-challenged buddies than to worry about what might happen today.

"Is your dad feeling okay enough to march?" I asked.

"Nah. He's riding with one of the news wagons in the back. It makes him as cranky as a hibernating bear, so I've come to march with you. If it's okay."

He pitched the question to Dad, who'd just come up. I could see my father processing Nick's request and thinking that it wasn't correct since he wasn't dressed in mourning like the rest of us. "Mr. Kawalsky can't walk because of what happened," I explained.

The appeal to family honor did it. "We'll be glad to have you march with us," Dad said. Then he turned away, asking irritably, "What's holding us up? Why aren't we starting the march?"

We found out when Senator Buford arrived ten minutes later with two aides in tow. He wore a well-fitting silk suit and posed for the cameras twice as he walked over to shake Dad's hand.

"Great photographic opportunity," Nick muttered, as cameras whirred.

"You don't like the good senator?" Alice asked under cover of the noise. "He's got a *great* profile."

Nick shrugged. "He's no worse than anyone else in politics, I guess." Then he added, "Uh, oh—here comes trouble."

Jerry Cho had finally made his appearance. His followers cheered and applauded loudly. Jerry said a few words to his group and then began to distribute headbands with "APU" written on them in big red letters.

"Mitch!" Damon suddenly called. "Mitch Mizuno!" Then, as Mitch turned, Damon flipped a headband through the air at him. "What a pass," he called. "What a catch!"

"What's he think—this is a football game?" But Nick's remark was drowned out as the drummer began to pound his drum.

"Now," Dad said sternly. "Are we ready, children? Remember that this is for your brother. For Harris."

Boom, boom, boom, mourned the drum ahead of us. "Mitch," Dad summoned.

Our younger brother left us and went to walk between Mom and Dad. As he did so, he slid his APU headband around his head. He looked around half defiantly, but nobody said anything. As planned, Alice and I fell in behind our folks and Mitch. Nick dropped into step beside me as we began to walk the sidewalk that ran along the perimeter of the Common.

It was strange. Although the band played loudly and the marchers shouted their various slogans, though traffic whooshed by on Charles Street outside the Common, inside me there was a heavy, cold stillness. The kind of stillness you sometimes feel just before a thunderstorm.

That ominous, waiting feeling intensified as we passed the old cemetery. Was it just my hyperactive imagination that made me think that unfriendly eyes were watching every step we took?

I kept a watchful eye out, but there was nothing suspicious to be seen. Not in the Common, not on busy Tremont Street. Not near the State House on Beacon either, where a lot of people had gathered to watch us on this warm June morning. Here police were busy rerouting traffic, and I felt a little better. The SAW surely wouldn't cause trouble with the cops around.

But the sun that glinted down on the gold dome of the State House was hot, and perspiration gathered under the collar of my black dress and pooled under my arms. My back itched.

"I'm boiling," Alice complained.

Boom, boom, boom, the drums thundered.

"Remember Harris Mizuno!" Damon's voice crested above even the threnody of the drums. I glanced back over my shoulder, and then stopped in my tracks because I'd caught a glimpse of Melanie Reed amongst the marchers.

Mel was marching for Harris, too—marching in spite of what she'd said about Waring. But before I could take in all of that thought, Nick grabbed my arm and hissed, "Look who's come to join the parade."

My heart sank as I saw that Link Lewis, together with a bunch of other guys, had muscled their way to the front row of onlookers. They were all wearing the racist badge with the fist and the sword.

I glanced over my shoulder again to see if the APU had noticed Link's presence, but there were too many marchers between us and Jerry Cho's group. "There aren't a whole lot of them," I said hopefully.

"They're around." Nick was looking up and down the swelling ranks of spectators. "Maybe Link's buddies don't want to be too visible yet. Maybe they're waiting for the moment when they'd cause the most damage and get the most publicity, like when the senator makes his speech."

"So you think these crazy racists are going to attack us then?" Alice asked. She sounded both indignant and nervous. Nick said that the SAW wouldn't have to push too hard to set Jerry and his boys off the deep end.

While Nick was still talking, Alice's nervousness increased. "We have to tell the folks," she exclaimed. "Get them to stop the parade."

I caught my sister's arm and turned her around. As far as we could see was a long, coiling snake of people. "See that?" I demanded. "How is anyone going to stop this march, huh? Besides, Mom and Dad knew there could be trouble. Reverend Thanh warned them."

"Probably nothing much will happen," Nick said in his most reasonable tone. "Unless—" He hesitated until Alice told him to quit stalling and spit it out. "Unless somebody pulls a knife or a gun," he then added.

Karo, standing on the corner of the street cocking his finger at me, silently pulling a mocking trigger. *Bang, bang, you're dead.* "But—but anyone shooting anyone in this crowd would be arrested," I protested.

"Cho's a fanatic," Nick said, "and racists eat up publicity. Silcom'd make a big deal about his 'martyrs for the cause of racial purity,' never mind if they did land in jail."

"That's it—I'm *out* of here," Alice exclaimed. "I don't care what Dad says—I am *not* going to stick around and get killed by crazies on *both* sides."

She pushed out of the line of marchers and started hiking back across the Common. Nick and I exchanged glances, and he said, "She won't get far before she changes her mind and comes back."

I wasn't sure whether I wanted Alice to come back. In many ways I wished I could go with her. I'd almost decided to follow her sensible example until I saw my kid brother walking between my father and mother. Foolish or not, I couldn't just take off and abandon my family.

Apparently Alice couldn't, either. Ten minutes later,

Nick broke silence to say, "What'd I tell you? Here she comes now."

My sister was running across the Common toward us. "Terri," she shouted, "you have to come with me. Now."

She grabbed hold of my arm and started pulling me back out of line and through the Common. "Hey," I protested, "what's the matter with you?"

"Just come," my sister hissed. Then, since it was obvious I wasn't about to move she added, "It's Obaachan."

"Obaachan?" I started to run after her, and Nick followed us both. "What's happened to Obaachan?"

Without a word, Alice led us out of the Common. "Look" I told her, "if this is some kind of trick—"

And then I dried up because I'd spotted a familiar Buick wagon parked near a roadblock on the corner of Charles and Boylston Streets. "What are the Blankards doing down here?" I demanded.

Then, I saw Obaachan. She was sitting in the front seat next to Art Blankard, and she had on the black kimono that she'd worn to come to America and a wide, white cotton band tied around her head. White strips of cloth crisscrossed her chest and were tied at the back.

"What's going on?" I practically yelled.

Art Blankard leaned out of the window to rumble, "Mama-san changed her mind about coming to march today. She came over and asked us to drive her here, so we did. We were stopped at this roadblock when we saw Alice coming out of the Common."

"I *told* Obaachan there was going to be trouble." Alice's voice cracked with agitation as she went on, "I *told* her she had to go home right away. But she won't move. All she said was that she wanted to talk to you."

I ran around to the passenger's seat where Obaachan sat, her face serious and determined, her small hands clasped on her lap. "You shouldn't have

166

come here, Obaachan. Alice is right. There'll be all kinds of trouble, soon—"

"That is why I come," Obaachan interrupted. "I ask Blankard-san bring me. I want go where Juntaro is."

"She wants to be with her family," Emily whinnied from the rear seat. "I mean, who can blame her? Here all of you are marching, and it's for Harris, who was such a great kid. So when your grandma came over, I said to Art, we can't sit still and not help because of a silly misunderstanding—"

"So, now what?" Art interrupted. "Do we take Mama-san home or do what she wants?"

Just then, a policeman who'd been rerouting traffic came over to tell us to move it along. Art looked at me, and I looked at Obaachan who begged, "I must be with Juntaro, Terri-chan."

I moistened my dry lips. "I'm Terri Mizuno, Officer, and this is my grandmother from Japan." I glanced nervously at Obaachan adding, "She—she needs to be with my family at the speakers' platform, but she can't walk clear across the Common."

"What're the chances of my dropping her off near the State House?" Art added.

The policeman looked at Obaachan, who put her hands together in a praying gesture and bowed her head. "Okay," he decided, "go up Charles, take a right on Beacon. But you can't park there, understand? The area's closed to traffic."

"Get in," Art said to us. I tumbled in next to Emily, and Alice and Nick followed. Squashed between Emily and my sister, I asked Obaachan what had made her change her mind about coming today, and she mumbled something that sounded like, *"Kataki uchi."*

"Revenge," Emily translated. "That means revenge, honey. I know because I asked her what it meant on our way down here. See, everybody wants revenge on somebody else. Everyone concerned wants to strike out at somebody for some*thing*. Your grandma can't stand it anymore."

Confused, I shot a look at Nick, who was nodding as if he understood. "What will you do, Mrs. Mizuno?" he asked.

Obaachan didn't answer. She bowed her gray head and looked down at her hands. "She's afraid there may be violence," Emily whispered loudly. "She's afraid her family will be hurt."

"Not afraid other peoples hurt them," Obaachan corrected suddenly. "Afraid they hurt *themselves*."

As she spoke, we arrived at another roadblock near the State House. Art spoke to the officer in charge and was instructed to pull up near the stone stairs that led down into the Common.

"The speakers' platform's just left of the stairs," Art rumbled. "You kids going to be okay taking Mama-san from here? I've got to go park this thing."

"I'll help." Emily hopped off spryly, pulled open the passenger door. "Come on, dear, easy does it now."

Looking as if she could barely put one foot in front of the other, Obaachan alighted. As she did so, Ms. Ziegler's powerful contralto voice rose in "America the Beautiful."

Turning from Obaachan, I looked down at the Common below us. All the marchers had gathered around the speakers' platform and were listening to the music. The folks and Mitch, Senator Buford and the clergy were on the platform standing with their backs to us.

But not everyone was entranced with Ms. Ziegler's paean to peace and brotherhood. I noticed that Link Lewis and his pals were no longer alone. A large number of guys, all wearing the racist badge, had infiltrated the crowd that'd gathered to watch the marchers.

Obaachan had clutched my hand and was pulling me toward the stone steps that led down into the Common. "Are you sure you want to do this?" I asked.

My grandmother's reply was drowned out by applause that followed the song. Now Rev. Thanh was on his feet explaining why we'd all gathered to march and why the tragedy that happened to Harris must never, never occur again.

"It's going to happen, though—right now it's going to," Alice groaned as Obaachan began heading for those stairs. "Why does the old woman have to be so stubborn?"

I didn't know why. All I knew was that the small, thin hand that gripped mine was strong with determination. We climbed down the stairs, and Obaachan gestured to the platform. "Take me that place, Terri-chan."

Emily Blankard, Nick, and Alice had kept up with us but stopped at the platform stairs. I made one last attempt. "Obaachan," I said, "are you sure you want to go up there? There are people out there who want to hurt us. Look what they did to Mitch and Nick and me."

"Shikataganai," Obaachan said.

Leaning heavily on me, she started up the stairs. Nobody paid much attention to us since even Mom was looking at Rev. Thanh, who'd finished his speech and was extolling the next speaker, Senator Buford.

"Here is a man who is courageous when speaking for his beliefs," he intoned. "Here is a public servant who does not shrink from the difficult and the dangerous. He is here today to stand shoulder to shoulder with us in shared grief for Harris Mizuno. With joy I give you—"

That was when he spotted Obaachan. He stopped dead in midsentence, and Senator Buford, who had begun to get up from his seat, sank down again.

"Okaa-san!" Dad exclaimed.

He jumped to his feet and started to walk over to her, but she waved him back and said something in rapid Japanese. Then she bowed to Rev. Thanh. "Excuse, please," she told him. "Must talk people now."

Rev. Thanh was so astonished that he stared at her pop-eyed. "Terri, what's this all about?"

169

I shook my head. "It wasn't my idea," I said to Dad, who was scowling at me. "She wanted to come."

"Japs, go home where you belong!"

No telling where that hoarse voice came from, but amongst the marchers I saw Jerry Cho stiffen to attention. He rapped out some order, and the APU began to fan out. Damon went with them.

This was the trouble Jerry had expected, and he was welcoming it. It was going to happen just as Nick had said. My stomach went into a pretzel twist as I saw a clump of shaven-headed guys step out of the crowd of onlookers.

"Waring didn't go far enough—he shoulda killed all you mongreloids!"

Mad as a hornet, Mitch hopped to his feet, but Mom pulled him back. I could see that she was trying to reason with him as Dad came over to us.

"Mother," he begged, "please sit down."

Instead of listening, Obaachan let go of my hand, walked forward, and stood facing the crowd. "Stop!" she cried. "You must not do this thing."

Her thin, frail voice rose like spray on the wind and was dashed aside. No one heard. Throwing out her arms, she went on desperately, "It is not right to hate anybody. Hating is evil!"

She broke off, turned to me. There was a plea in her eyes. *Terri-chan, help me.*

Hardly thinking of what I was doing, I grabbed the mike from Rev. Thanh's hand and shoved it close to Obaachan's face. "You must stop," she repeated, and this time her voice took off. She backed off from the mike, surprised at the sound of her voice, but then edged close to add, "The hating must stop."

"What are you talking about, you old bat?" a skinhead standing up in front jeered.

"Shut up, you big bozo!" Mitch broke away from Mom and ran down the stairs, but Nick grabbed him and hung on. "Lemme go," Mitch shouted, struggling and raging. "I'll get them for what they did to Harris."

170

"This march no more for Harrisu." Above the noise Obaachan spoke sternly. "Not for Harrisu. This march not for my grandson. No more. It has become full of people with hate in their hearts."

Dad had his hand on Obaachan's arm. She wouldn't budge. "Tell your mother that she has to leave, *now*," Rev. Thanh practically wept.

Obaachan looked scared to death, but she was also determined. She grabbed the microphone from me and gripped it tightly in her shaking hand.

She wasn't about to leave the platform till she'd had her say. I'd never seen anybody braver than that old lady. Remembering how Obaachan had worked her fingers bloody to feed her kids during the war, I actually snarled at the reverend, who was trying to get her to sit down. "Leave her alone," I snapped.

"Yes, let her have her say," I heard a familiar voice declare and realized that Mom had risen to her feet. She walked across the platform to us and stood beside Obaachan. "She has the right to speak."

Mom was talking to the reverend but she looked straight at Dad as she spoke. For a second they just looked at each other, and then Dad cleared his throat. "My wife is right. Let my mother say what she has to," he said.

Then he, too, stepped up beside Obaachan and me. Meanwhile someone in the crowd called, "Let the old lady have her say!"

People began to cheer. The antiviolence group members raised their signs and shook them. Somebody in the crowd began to clap, and others joined the rhythmic beat of approval.

Obaachan raised her head, opened her mouth—and nothing came out. With everyone's attention on her, she was scared, spitless. "Terri-chan," she gasped, "I—I don't know what to say. In English I have not words."

"If she hesitates, she'll lose them," Rev. Thanh warned, and I knew he was right.

"We'll tell them together," I vowed. "It's for Harris, Obaachan. You're here because of Harris, remember?"

The fear didn't leave her face, but the determination came back. She once more turned to the crowd and raised her voice to say, "I am Mizuno Sachiko, grandmother of Harrisu. I come from Japan. I never see my grandson Harrisu because of hate."

There were shouts of "Waring," but she shook her head. "Not Waring. He not responsible for why I never see Harrisu. Man who was responsible, who had hate in his heart, was my husband."

What was she talking about? Was she all right in the head? What's this about her husband? The whispers, the mutters went around but fell gradually silent when Obaachan started to tell the story of my grandfather Mizuno and his hatred of America. Often she paused to look at me, and I'd give her the word she needed, but it was her quavery old voice that held the crowd.

"My husband was too much full of hate." She put her hand to her heart. "He hate his son, so he would not see grandchildren. Ah, he shut his face, shut heart, to Juntaro and Juntaro's family. Hate destroy him like fire."

She drew a deep breath. "Here, today, I see such hate again."

Someone—a SAW sympathizer, probably—made a rude noise, but Obaachan had the crowd now. I could see them hanging on her words, listening to her as she said that revenge never helped or healed.

"Revenge make things more bad. Love build up; revenge break down." Obaachan paused to pull in a breath. "Today, here is many people. Old people, young people. Some with shaved heads think only white people are good, other people should be sent away from America. Other ones with white *hachimaki* around heads think Asians should be strongest of all. White *hachimaki* and shaved heads want to fight each other, but not because of Harrisu. They want to fight because they have hate in hearts."

As if to underscore her words, a scuffle broke out in the crowd. APU versus the Brotherhood of the SAW— but before it could escalate, I saw a cadre of plain-clothes men and women close in on the troublemakers and move them right out. The police had been there in the crowd all the time.

Now Obaachan stopped speaking and turned to me. "Terri-chan," she said, "read."

She was stuffing something into my hands—my essay on hatred. "I can't read this," I exclaimed, and she looked me straight in the eye.

"For Harrisu," she commanded.

Breath soured in my throat, and my stomach gave such a jolt I thought I would throw up. Obaachan stuffed the microphone into my limp hand. *Do* it.

"You write good things. Say in English what I feel." She put her small hand on her heart. "Say what in *here*, Terri-chan. Say for Harrisu."

Big brother, I hope you appreciate this. Was there, somewhere in my mind, the ghost of that remembered chuckle? Shaking all over with nerves, I stepped up to the mike, lifted the sheet of paper, and began, "I am so sick of hate."

I tried to concentrate on the words I'd written so that I wouldn't have to be aware of anyone or anything else. But I knew all those people were there— people who no doubt sympathized with the skinheads and who had come to join in making trouble, people who were marching because they themselves had lost loved ones to violence, people like Melanie and the Blankards who had come because deep down they'd remained our friends.

"—And a million grains of soot will kill the plant forever," I read. "We have to stop before we kill everything that is decent and good in ourselves."

There was a silence. In it I could hear flags flapping

in the wind, a baby crying. Obaachan nodded at me to continue, and I read the final paragraph.

"My brother Harris was a special human being. He brought joy to his family and friends. All of us loved him. And yet every day we lose Harris again and again. How can this be, you ask? It's because our Harris dies again every time someone's son, or brother, or mother, or sister, or friend is killed through hate and bigotry and violence."

I broke off, losing my battle with tears. Obaachan leaned forward, speaking into the mike. With her hand tightly clasping mine she said, "Please, remember my grandson. Cry for him. But give his death some—" She broke, fumbled for words, turned to me.

"Some dignity," I said through the tears that were streaming down my cheeks. "Give his death some dignity."

"Give his death some dignity," Obaachan repeated, and suddenly, her thin old voice was stern with power. "Must not let hating people use my grandson as excuse to hurt and kill. Hate must not again destroy someone else."

TWELVE

DAD HAD BEEN standing beside Obaachan all this time. Now, she took a step backward and they faced each other. From the way he looked at her, I thought Dad might put his arms around his mother. Instead he bowed very deeply and kept his head down until she reached out and touched his shoulder. "Jun-chan," she murmured.

My dad straightened and turned to me, and I saw that there were tears in his eyes. Then he bowed to *me*. Bowed deep and low.

"Terri," he said, "forgive me. You were right and I was wrong."

So I cried all over again, and he hugged me, and Mom hugged us both *and* Obaachan, too, and then Alice ran up onto the platform, and finally even Mitch got into the act—though later he flatly denied it and said no way would he have acted like such a geeky weirdo in front of three thousand people.

Obaachan's speech put a different spin on the solidarity march. Being trained as a clergyman, though, Rev. Thanh immediately jumped on the bandwagon and, quoting Corinthians, spoke about the redemptive power of love in such a fine, beautiful voice that a lot of people were in tears.

Not to be left behind, Senator Buford threw out his prepared text and plunged into an eloquent speech about brotherhood and love casting out suspicion and hatred. "We are all immigrants in this country," the senator declared. "We are all brothers and sisters, so there's no room to hate anyone. We must never forget that we are all human."

During this stirring speech, I learned later, plain-clothes officers were quietly patrolling the area ejecting anyone who even looked as though he or she might start trouble. Due to their efforts, by the time we headed for the State House, there wasn't a shaved head or an APU headband in sight. Jerry Cho had vanished, and I didn't see Damon, either. Those APU members who'd stuck around had removed their headbands and now stood around listening with a dazed look in their eyes.

Usually, the governor sent a delegate to accept petitions, but today he himself came out onto the State House steps. He even shook Obaachan's hand, and she bowed so low that she almost toppled over.

"It was his *excellency* the *governor* of Mass-a-chu-setts," she kept repeating in the car when, an hour later, we headed toward home. "Is unbelievable—so honorable person has shaked my hand!"

But she was drooping by the time we got home, which caused a problem. The Mizunos were guests of honor at the after-march party that Rev. Thanh had organized at the South Street Unitarian Church. "It will look bad if we don't go," Mom said, when Dad suggested hopefully that we could all stay home. "After all that happened today, we must at least show our faces."

Agreeing that it would be impolite not to go, Dad added, "But one of us has to stay with Mother. I don't want her to be left alone."

So I volunteered to stay with Obaachan. It was a relief, in a way, not having to talk and shake hands, to say and hear the same thing over and over. Anyway, I needed time to think about what had happened today, about how one little old lady had stood up and said, "Enough!" and how three thousand people had listened to her.

When I told Mom I really didn't mind staying home,

she hugged me tight. "I don't think I could have been as brave as that old lady was today," she said, and I knew it was *Mom* talking again—the old, decisive, forthright Mom who had burst out of her own shadows right there on the speaker's platform today. "And, Terri, you were pretty darn brave, too. I'm proud of you." She paused and added softly but firmly, "Harris would be, too."

Are you, Harris? I asked him in the silence that remained behind with me after my family had left. As usual, there was no answer, and I knew that thinking of my big brother had been a mistake. Now that I didn't have my anger and hate to keep it at bay, the old ache came back and with it the terrible sense of loss.

Too restless to stay still, I went upstairs and checked on a fast-asleep Obaachan, and then went downstairs to get myself a soda from the fridge. But just as I was reaching for one, the doorbell rang.

If that was another reporter, I'd tell him to go chase himself—but when I'd stomped over to the door and opened it, there was Damon Ying. Since Damon was the last person I'd ever expected to see, I just gaped at him until he went, "Hi, Terri. Can I come in?"

"My grandmother's asleep," I said. "I don't want to wake her."

That wasn't the whole truth. The truth was that I didn't *want* to be alone with Damon. The memory of what had happened in the park was still too vivid, and so was the memory of the night Karo had beaten us up. "What do you want?" I asked.

"Just to tell you that it took guts to get up on that speakers' platform today." I said my grandmother was a spunky lady, and he said, "I'm talking about, you."

"The last time we talked," I blurted, "you called me a coward."

Damon flushed. "I said a few things I didn't mean," he admitted. "Seeing Waring in the park—you under-

177

stand how I felt, right? I wanted to avenge Harris's death."

"By terrorizing an old man?"

He frowned. "Are we talking about the same guy, here? That 'old man' murdered your brother." When I said nothing he added, "Jerry's right—women just don't understand."

"This woman doesn't, for sure," I snapped back, and Damon's frown deepened. This wasn't the Terri Mizuno he'd known, his friend's tongue-tied, adoring kid sister.

Suddenly, he smiled at me. "Hey, let's not fight, pretty girl."

I waited for a flip of my heart, some small stir of what I'd once felt for Damon. Instead, as I looked at this handsome, dark-eyed guy I'd practically worshiped all year, I realized something.

Damon wasn't as tall as I'd thought he was. His shoulders weren't as broad. And his look of self-assurance wasn't attractive—it was just plain smug.

"Tell me," I said, "did you and Jerry Cho see Karo and his pals chase us down Ferndale that night?" Damon's eyes narrowed. "I thought maybe you had a chance to stop them beating on us but didn't."

Outrage—indignation—and then alarm flared in his eyes. So Nick had been right, I thought as Damon snapped, "Who told you that damned lie?"

Silently, I listened as he blustered how off base I was. He then added that Jerry was leaving Westriver for New York, where he apparently had friends.

"It's the damned cops—they're putting heat on the wrong guy as usual. I hate to see him go," Damon went on gloomily. "Jerry's taught me more in a few weeks than I've learned in all my life. And he gets results, man. We caught those punks who beat you up, remember?"

He gazed at me reproachfully, trying to shame me into apologizing. But instead of retreating into tongue-tied remorse, I met Damon's gaze straight on.

"Did Jerry teach you that the end justifies the means?"

Damon's flush bled away, leaving him almost pale under his tan. "It's not you talking that kind of crap," he jerked out. "It's that geek, that Kawalsky. He's messing you in the head, filling it with garbage."

"Just so's you know," I retorted, "it's my head and it's no garbage."

"Well, hey, if you can think something like that about me, there's no use talking," he said. He started to swing away, then paused to give me what probably was supposed to be a reproachful, melting look. "I thought we were friends." Damon sighed.

Once, I'd have died happy just seeing that look. The thought of being Damon's *friend* would have caused me to jump rings around the moon. Now, I just noted that my former hero didn't actually walk like a jungle cat. He swaggered.

"I already have a friend," I told him.

And then I shut the door.

"Are you sure you have to go?" I asked for about the fiftieth time. "You could stay through the summer. It's cooler here in Westriver than in Japan, you said."

Obaachan paused in the act of folding her kimonos into the old suitcase. "I like heat," she said.

"Besides, I'd be home during the summer, and we could hang out—do stuff together," I added.

"We have done many stuffs." My grandmother held up one small hand and began to count. "We have done the aquarium and the Omni Theater. We have gone to the church picnic. We have driven to Ar-i-su's university. We have gone many place."

Her eyes lit up. Obaachan had truly enjoyed traveling to Vermont and New Hampshire and Maine. It was, Alice and I agreed, as if that day at Boston Common had changed her, freed her to have fun.

"Much fun I had," Obaachan went on. "But now

179

time to go back to Japan, stay very quiet in one place, and think of all stuffs we have done."

I trailed my fingers up and down my bedspread. "I guess you must miss your grandchildren in Japan."

"I miss," she admitted, and I felt a small twinge of something like jealousy. *Whoa*, I told myself. It was normal that my grandmother should miss the only family her husband had allowed her to have. If things had been different, I'd have gone back and forth to Japan with Mitch and Alice and Harris—

"But I miss you, too," Obaachan was saying, "and Mitch-chan and A-ri-su. Too much I miss."

If I'd thought that one day I'd feel bad about her leaving—her and her spirit altar (now packed away) and that little bell and all her lectures about my behavior, I'd have thought myself crazy.

"I'll miss you, too," I told her honestly.

There was a knock on the door and Mitch poked his nose in. "The Kawalskys are here, and the Blankards are coming over to say good-bye," he announced. "I can hear Emily squawking from here."

Because those fences had been mended. Art Blankard had explained to Dad that he had never agreed to be interviewed by any scummy tabloid paper. He'd sworn he hadn't been paid a damned cent, either. Emily had been rattling her gums to that big-mouthed Despard woman, had allowed that she was worried that the SAW might come back, and Mrs. Despard, not Emily, had talked to a reporter.

"I agree Emily's got a big mouth but tabloids don't have any shame," Art had rumbled, when he and Dad had finished apologizing to each other. "They lie all the time. Maybe, Jun, you and me can sue the sumbitching paper," he'd added hopefully.

So peace in the neighborhood had been restored, and since Obaachan was leaving in the morning, Mom had asked the Blankards over. And she had invited the Kawalskys, too.

We went down the stairs to the beginnings of a

party. Emily hugged Obaachan and gave her a bunch of useless gifts. "You've got younger since you came to Westriver," Emily insisted.

Actually for once Emily was right. Obaachan did look younger because she wasn't wearing black anymore. Not long after the day of the solidarity march, Mom, Alice, and I'd taken her shopping and introduced her to the discount stores after which our grandmother had never been the same. The dress she was wearing now (petite size two) was a pretty royal blue with sprays of white flowers on it, selected by that queen of style, Alice Mizuno herself. The dress took twenty years off Obaachan, especially now, when she was laughing at something Art was saying.

Alice drew me aside. "Obaachan's enjoying herself," she said. "At least this way she can't be in the kitchen getting in Mom's hair." She paused. "I can't believe the change in her. Remember when she first came?"

"Maybe we changed, too," I said, and my sister nodded, suddenly somber.

"I wonder *why* all the time. *Why* did Harris have to go out for mayonnaise that night? Why did Wenstein's have to be out of it?"

What was the point in wondering? I asked myself as Mom called Alice over to help her. I would miss Harris till the day I died, and our family could never be whole and together as it had been before, but there was no use looking over your shoulder. Life pushed you forward.

Pushed you on to outgrow and end some old relationships and to try and repair others. Take Melanie Reed and me, for instance. Seeing her march for Harris had helped mend the break between us, and we were friends again. Maybe our friendship wouldn't be as strong as before—maybe it would just be different. Friendships changed, just as people did.

Obaachan had taught me that. I looked at that old lady and knew, suddenly, that I was going to write about her. Write about her from the heart, I mean,

181

letting words I couldn't get past my tongue soar out of me on paper. Like songbirds at first light—

"Are you thinking or feeling sick?" Kawalsky had come over to stand by me. "Your eyes are crossed."

He grinned so infectiously that I laughed. Kawalsky wasn't by any stretch handsome, and he was as skinny as a grasshopper and his cowlick would always fall into his glasses, but I was glad he was there. Strange but true, when Nick was around, I always felt good.

He was going on, "So, did you hear the news? Karo got bailed out of jail and he's disappeared, along with the so-called Society of Aryan Warriors sent here from Louisiana." I asked, what about Link? "I heard that he's got to go to court for assaulting a police officer. It's *over* for the so-called white supremacists—for now, anyway."

"Whoever named them supremacists?" I wondered. "Harris would say that they were supreme jerks."

There was a slight cough behind me, and I saw Dad standing there. At the sound of Harris's name, I saw the familiar barrier rising in his eyes, but then he seemed to shake himself free of it.

Totally deadpan he said, "No, he wouldn't. He'd say they were supreme *asses*."

Kawalsky winced, but I laughed—more from relief that Dad wasn't going to crawl back into his shell again than at his awful pun.

"Harris liked puns," Alice added, from across the room. Her smile had as much amusement as sorrow as she added, "He liked to take words and see how far he could stretch them. Like you guys used to do with your dumb game, Terriyaki."

I couldn't believe that we were actually talking about Harris openly. It was painful, but it also felt good, like the itch that comes when a deep wound is finally healing over.

Just then there was another ring on the doorbell, and Kurt Shih walked in. "I'm not staying," he said, shaking hands with Dad and Mom. "I just came by to wish Mrs. Mizuno, Sr., a safe trip and to tell you the news. Ms. Fallister has been fired by her former client."

"Waring fired her?" Mom breathed. "But why?"

"He *says* that he's had enough of her tricks, that he wants to face up to what he did. *I* feel that his new attorney wants desperately to make a deal." He paused and added, "Don't worry, we won't plead it down. Waring's going to do it all."

While Mr. Shih was talking, I noticed that Obaachan had moved closer to Dad. She didn't touch him or anything, but she looked at him intently.

Kurt Shih was saying, "I was looking forward to beating Grace Fallister in court." Regret for lost publicity tinged his voice as he added, "But we can still make an example of Waring."

"Then do so," Dad snapped. "I'll never forgive the man who murdered my son. I'll never forgive, never forget—"

Obaachan coughed, softly, behind her hand. Dad looked at her, and the anger dimmed in his eyes. "But I don't want my son's death to turn into any personal vendetta or crusade," he went on heavily. "Time was, I'd have been glad to strangle Waring with my own hands. Now—now I'm willing to let the law take its course."

"I'll drink to that." Mr. Shih looked somber for a second, and then unexpectedly turned to me.

"Terri, I understand you've got your heart set on law," he said. "I could put you in touch with a friend in private practice. She takes a few bright young people each year and lets them do a mini-apprenticeship so they can get a feel of what law is really about." He paused. "She's a gifted attorney and a master teacher. Time spent with her would be gold."

I could feel the whole weight of the room's attention on me. Dad's eyes widened, and I could almost hear his mind working. Terri apprenticing with a famous attorney? Unbelievable but wonderful news! The fumble-tongued klutz of the family had finally done something right, something to make him proud of her.

"That sounds good, Mr. Shih," Dad said. He smiled at me and added, "It's a great opportunity, Terri."

Mitch did a thumbs-up gesture, Alice did a silent rah-rah thing with both hands, and Mom was so pleased she got red in the face. "Oh, Terri, how wonderful! What a chance for you! What do you say to Mr. Shih?"

"Actually," I heard my voice saying, "I don't think I want to go into law. I'd like to try being a writer."

Even as the words were leaving my lips, I regretted them. My cheeks burned as I saw Kurt Shih look at my astounded parents. Then, a little too heartily he said, "Oh, right. That's fine, then."

Alice rolled her eyes at me and silently drew a finger across her throat. "But, Terri," Mom gasped, as Mr. Shih said his farewells and left the house, "*Why?* You always said—"

"It was more like you and Dad always said," I mumbled. Everybody was listening while pretending not to listen, and I was feeling totally embarrassed. "Look, please can we talk about this later?"

"Writing," Mom said, shaking her head. She started to walk away, came back to demand, "Why *writing*, all of a sudden?"

"She write good things," Obaachan said, supporting me. "Terri-chan have a good hand with word."

Mr. Kawalsky added from the table, where he was helping himself to the food, "You can do an apprenticeship on the *Herald* anytime, Terri."

I glanced at Dad wondering when he was going to blast me. His forehead was puckered into a frown, and the line of his mouth was ominous. "A *writer*," Mom said again, as if she couldn't take it in. Poor Mom, who'd had her heart set on her daughter being appointed a Supreme Court justice one day. "What